GRGAT
STORY.

D.J. FAIR.

BOOK U.U. GOOD

1968

$ 1200

The Jinker

THE
JINKER

a novel by
JOSEPH SCHULL

1968
Macmillan of Canada   Toronto
Macmillan & Co Ltd   London

Printed in Canada for
The Macmillan Company of Canada Limited
70 Bond Street, Toronto
by Maracle Press Limited

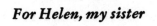

For Helen, my sister

The Jinker

T HE stone's grey face had been streaked by a winter's rain, pocked by the north-west sleets. There was dirty snow in the chiselled troughs of the letters:

ELIJAH TORRANCE
Born July 9, 1819
Lost in the Ice
March 19, 1890

Here in the raw wet and fitful sunlight of another March afternoon it said nothing and it stirred nothing. It grew from the mud and slush with the other stones, bleak as the gull-cries, mute as the bare hill, and there were no bones under it. Robert Torrance put his cap back on his head and turned away.

'Well? Are ye ready to give over now?' The old man moved at his side, dour and half forgotten. Torrance made no answer. They came out by the scrubby, wind-whipped trees at the graveyard gate, and he stood for a moment glowering down at the sea. He was not yet ready to meet those hard blue eyes.

Ernest Johns had been a year older or a year younger than his father; Torrance could never remember which it was. The two had sailed together for forty years, master and mate. To Johns, the son in the father's place was still a boy, but he was a master now too and expected to behave as one. There was no trace of the ways of Elijah Torrance in this bucketing about St. John's on the day before sailing-day. A sealer's captain belonged on his own deck, remote with his own concerns. This one, high on the hill here after the rowdy port, was making a spectacle of himself. Johns was moodily angry because he was

3

part of the spectacle too, dogged and understanding, not to be shaken off.

All through the dismal, useless, wasted hours he had refused to go back to the ship, refused to leave Torrance's side. With a thousand chores to be seen to on their own vessel, they had sculled round the harbour climbing to the decks of others, soon with a wash of rumour running ahead of them. The eyes of the captains had glinted with understanding as they came over the sides, the men on the decks had edged away for the hatches. They had cornered little groups in the holds and 'tween-decks, and watched them dissolve with shifting eyes and shrugs. They had combed the quaysides and stood in the warehouse doorways, stopping impatient stragglers hurrying for the last berths. They had not missed a foot of the dozen stinking lanes that twisted up from the water. Grog shops, chandlers' shops, the shops of the haggling whores – wherever the sea-boots squelched or a door swung or a coin clanked or a drink went down they had elbowed in with the question. To be met with the sudden quiet, the glint that told too much, the answer that told nothing.

'Well now, lads,' – Torrance had been the affable captain for as long as he could manage it – 'all of you here again, I see, and all ready for the hunt. Would it happen that any of you sailed last year in *Kestrel?*' And when the looks passed and the answer came as always: 'Well then, could you tell me where I might find a man who did?'

It was only at the fag end of the search, in the last and muckiest of the taverns, that he had lost his grip on himself. He had pushed at the rotting timbers of a crazy door, stepped down on sweating stone, and stood with Johns for a moment in the reek of rum and pipe smoke. The heads at the crowded tables had turned his way, the racket of boozy laughter had died out. The mugs had hovered respectfully, half-way to open mouths. All outport men; he could have called off a dozen of their names as he put the question and watched it settle among them like a stone in water. Killing the liquor again, he had thought grimly; and then, abruptly, it was too much. They were all a part of his doubts and fears and torment, these blank-eyed, stubbly oafs, shaking their sheep's heads. 'Liars, the lot of you!' he had heard

4

himself bellowing. 'Some of you've been going for seals as long as I have. You know the ships and you know the men aboard of 'em. D'ye mean to tell me there's not one man from *Kestrel* who's back in the port this year?'

The fingers of Ernest Johns had closed on his arm, steely and brusque, swinging him round toward the door. He had flung them off but he had gone, cursing and sick of himself, sick of the game. The bones in the ice meant nothing now, the stone on the hill meant nothing; his course was set as sure as tomorrow's sun. Yet he had pushed out from the pub with a sudden passionate hunger, fought his way like a blind man up the length of the riotous street, and, still with Johns beside him, climbed the path to the graveyard.

Now, as they stood together on the lip of the hill, the port sprawled out beneath them, linked by the rocky trail with Water Street at the bottom. The wind, which had lulled for a bit, cut clean and sharp again. Across the breadth of the oval harbour the cliffs of the South Side climbed in their lumpy terraces, shutting away the sea. To the left, below, along the jagged stretch of the shoreline, the bare birch poles of the flakes stood up, smelling of last year's fish and last year's salt. The gutting-tables were clear, most of them upside down to protect their tops from the weather. It would be a month yet before the schooners and dories began to come in, heaped to the gunwales with cod. There was no rank of chattering women, their arms red to the armpits, splitting and heading, gutting and salting. There were no shouting boys climbing about the flakes, laying out fat white halves to dry in the sun. Nobody thought of the flakes now. This was the month when schooners lay idle all around the coast, and the big, blunt-bowed sealers gathered in the oval harbour. Women and boys would be doing the chores in the outports, while St. John's seethed with fishermen who had forgotten fish for a while.

For two weeks the strangers who came each year had been flowing in, gaff in hand, pack on back, some by boat, some by the snowy bush-trails, some of them cutting down along the crackling shore ice. They had filled the chandlers' shops with the bustle of fitting out. The quays and the warehouse offices had

5

been one long, cheerful riot as town men scrambled with shore men for the berths in the best ships. It was nearly over now. Most of the fist-fights were done with, most of the berths claimed, and the soberer men were already aboard their vessels, keeping a watch on their gear. The ones who crowded the streets were the last lingerers, sure enough of their two-foot space in a hold but still restless. Duffle bags safely stowed, the knives at their belts fresh-honed, they were downing the good-luck drinks, building their nerve and hopes, talking of pelts and patches. And beyond the neck of the harbour and the circling ring of the cliffs the luck waited.

The quays below were lined with a straggle of ships, and a dozen more lay off, swinging at anchor. From amid the smoke and bustle Torrance could pick out the *Jean Bright*'s lanky funnel and bare masts. She was rubbing hulls and cross-trees with the rest of the pack, waiting for the morning gun. The best of the Bracebridge ships, and there were none better. To the port she was a Torrance ship, for no man but a Torrance had ever taken her to the ice. He knew her as he knew his own body, and he had given her better care. He had never looked at her, till this year, without pride and love and eagerness. Now she was as powerless to stir him as the grey stone in the graveyard. In this moment, out of enormous weariness, he would have given all he owned to be letting her go without him.

His eyes moved to *Kestrel*, black-hulled, heavy-bowed, swinging to her hook two cables' length away across the forest of masts and spars from *Jean Bright*. Her deck, the one deck in the fleet he had not gone near this day, was as crowded and busy as his own. For a moment he stiffened, tempted, but Johns had guessed the thought. 'No. You'll keep away from her. It's the one bit of sense you've shown.'

'Mahan might well be expecting me. He'll have heard the talk in the port.'

'He'll have heard, all right. He'll be grinning about it now. You've done his work for him, Robbie, better than he could himself.' The rich old voice, which almost sixty years of bellowing down the wind had not made hoarse, was heavy with reproof. 'You've stirred up the port, you've set the fleet on edge,

6

and you've found nothing. What was it all for?'

'For?' Torrance was bleak and curt. 'I lost my father in the ice last year. D'ye forget that? I'd like to know how he went.'

'And ye do know. Or ye think ye know. And it's not the cause of this traipsing about the port.'

'Is it not?' He could feel the anger rising, but it was a false anger. The old man's understanding scraped at his nerves. 'How would I find the truth, if not now? What other chance have I had? When *Kestrel* came back last year, the men scattered. She'd hardly a line made fast before they were up for their shares – grabbing their money and off – there was no holding 'em.'

Johns shrugged. 'Sealers at the end of a season – what d'ye expect of 'em? Specially the men in that ship. For five years now – longer than that – there's not been a man in the island hard enough or hungry enough to sail twice with him.'

'But they still come back for the hunt. They go in other ships. There's men from *Kestrel* scattered all through the fleet – and you know it!'

'I do.' Johns nodded. 'I saw 'em. I could have named a dozen of 'em – and what would be the good? There's nothing they know for sure, man – and they won't talk of what they think. They fill up with screech to forget it.'

Torrance was looking away, shaking his head. He struck a hand to his side with dogged quiet. 'There still could have been one man – just one. If I'd found one of his deck-watch, say, that had seen something, heard something –'

'You'd have done what? – laid a charge with the magistrates?'

'And why not?' He had caught the dour irony and felt it himself – he could not see Mahan in the grip of a town constable. But he went on. 'The magistrates would have been glad enough of a charge – so would the whole port. It would have been enough to haul him off that ship, hold him here. We'd be going north with another master in *Kestrel,* and no mischief brewing.'

'Too simple.' The irony was harder and bleaker in Johns's voice. 'It won't work, and you never hoped it would. You'll not

7

go down to his ship.' They were both moodily studying the commotion on the far-off deck. 'He's filled her up with strangers again, raw lads and the last scrapings from the outports – nothing to be learned from them.'

'I'm not saying there would be.' Torrance's voice was soft. 'But I'd find him aboard of her, and maybe we'd end things there.'

'Aye. It's been that in your mind all day, hasn't it? It's been back of all this foolery round the port. Listen to me, Robbie –' He waited, insistent, pleading.

'Well?'

'You'll not bring back your father with all this. And you'll not help yourself. There's nothing to be mended now with fists or a knife or a gaff.'

'Is there not?' Torrance turned on him. 'That'll be the way of it yet, Ernest, and you know it.'

'Do I?' The old man met his stare. 'How much d'ye want it, boy? How much would it help you?'

The old eyes saw too much. Torrance shrugged away from them. 'Better here than somewhere up in the ice. That was my real thought. If I'd roused him off that ship –'

'No.'

'No, is it? So I set up a stone in a graveyard, and all's done. Is that what ye think, Ernest? Is it what ye thought last year when we woke up in the ice?'

'It's no matter what I thought.' Johns was gruff and evasive. 'Or if it is, ye'll find it in Lije's Bible. It was lying on his cabin desk when I came down to look for him. He should have stayed by it.'

'Should he now? And why didn't he?' Torrance felt anger hardening in him again. 'No wind, no shift in the ice – nothing. We went to our bunks in the midst of a flat calm. You were the last man to see him at the start of the middle watch – you were up to the deck ahead of me in the morning – and you've no thoughts about it!'

'I said I've none that'll help anything now. Maybe they're the same as yours, some of 'em, but –'

'Aye, they are, all right, for you've asked the same questions. *How* did he go? Where? What took him from the ship

8

with no word to the watch, none to you, none to me? He'd come up from his cabin, hadn't he? And he'd heard something or he'd seen something – you know that. And he'd slipped over the side and dropped to the ice, alone out there in the stillness –' The picture rose in his mind, and for the first time that day the real grief surged with it, hot and stabbing. He turned away for a moment, quieting himself, seeing it all, hearing it – the ship and the sighing ice, the moonless dark, the high, cold stars, and the dawn – the dawn that broke at last, merciless and unrevealing. 'And no man of the deck-watch seeing where he went. And me asleep below.' He paused, looking at the harbour again. 'And Tim Mahan's *Kestrel* half a mile away.'

His eyes fastened on the squat bulk of the ship, darkening now as the shadows lengthened from the cliff. The name brooded on his tongue. 'Tim Mahan –'

Johns made no move for a moment, but he seemed to stand away. There was a new coldness and a new quiet in his voice as he pointed down to the harbour. 'Twenty good ships there, Robbie – near four thousand men. They're going to the ice for seals – to come back safe with the fat and go home with a little money. Nothing else.'

'Well?'

'You'll answer for one of those crews, and so will I. Maybe for more than one. They're not going to the ice to deal with Tim Mahan.'

'And if there's no choice?'

'You'll make the choice. You'll keep off from him.'

Torrance straightened and drew a breath, tall in the sunset glitter, smelling ice in the wind. 'If I can. If I go.'

'*If* you go?'

He stirred irritably under the anxious, searching eyes. 'You'd best get back to the ship. I've got to have a word with Bracebridge yet, and my gear's still at the house. I'll sleep there tonight.'

'But you'll be aboard in the morning.' It was not a question, it was not a hope. Whatever Torrance might say, whatever he said himself, Johns knew. They were all together and moving now like the ice in the great current.

9

I'VE been worried, Robert – I don't mind telling you that. It would be a sore blow to lose you.'

Torrance nodded, eyeing the glass in his hand. He was hardly listening.

'And I doubt if you'd help yourself if you left the trade. There's much ahead for you with us.' The island brogue was homely on the tongue of Simon Bracebridge, but the English schools of his boyhood had softened its rough edges. His speech was the speech of the big ones, the owners, the men who lived apart. Through a dozen generations the sea had built them, and spread the concerns of their lives as wide as the trade routes. They had taken the world for their province though they made the island their home, and they were men of the world first.

It did not make them strangers and it did not make them resented. Never before, Torrance thought, had he even known that sense of bigness and apartness. It had lain about him like the cliffs and the sea itself, a thing he lived with. All his kind had lived with it, through all those generations. It was only today that the thought of his kind oppressed him, angered him with a strange, dim, foreign anger. He could not look up from the wine-glass with its fragile crystal stem and the play of the amber light in its tilting bowl. As he turned it between his fingers he had never been so conscious of his great, strong awkwardness, of the sea smell and the fish smell that clung to the rough wool of his coat. He had never thought of his hands, gnarled and bent, scarred by bruising iron, splintering wood, rope and tar. Why was he thinking of them now, looking at them with the eyes of a resentful stranger?

He raised the glass to his lips and emptied it, quickly,

irritably. The sherry was dry and light and insipid on his tongue, a gentleman's drink, an old maid's tipple. Bracebridge leaned over with the decanter, mistaking impatience for thirst, and the wine climbed in the bowl again. Torrance eyed it, still with the secret scorn, but held it from his lips, carefully. Even in this, today, there was fire enough to set the raw tangle of his nerve ends blazing up like tinder.

'I could hardly imagine a ship of ours in the ice,' Bracebridge was saying, 'under any man but a Torrance. Nor could I imagine a Torrance giving up sealing. Yet there's been all this talk through the winter.'

'I know.' Torrance was still absorbed in the glass and its contents.

'*Had* you thought of giving it up?' The cool grey eyes, deep-set in the ruddy face under the frame of white hair, were searching, a little anxious. Torrance did not meet them but he knew the look. He had seen it now for more than eleven months, lurking in the eyes of every friend in the port.

'I'd thought of it.' He nodded. 'Yes. There are times when it seems the game's not worth the candle. A man could stay home and be near as well off in the end. It's a month lost from the fishing after all, and with my father gone —' He let it hang in the air. It was true enough though it said nothing. It did not come near his thoughts but it served for an answer. He could see the hint of relief in the grey eyes.

'Aye,' Bracebridge said, 'it was a hard blow that, for all of us. And it shakes a man to the roots, it unsettles him. You're one of the old line, Robert, anyway – a bit too big for the island, and the fishing on the Banks, and the short runs in the schooners. You'd be happiest in a big square-rigger, beating about the world.'

'Aye.'

'But those days are gone now. They'll not be back. So there's the fish trade and the wine trade left to us – and the seals, always the seals. It's a mucky business, getting 'em – always has been. I don't doubt there are times when a man's fed up with it. But it pays, and it can pay well in a good season.' He was on safe ground now; Torrance had marked it out for

12

him. He could talk of shares and money.

'It's been Bracebridges and Torrances together for as long
as anybody can remember, and I'd not want it changed. I think
we've dealt fairly with you in the past, but if sharing's a prob-
lem we'll not be behindhand. Your father's had ten shares and
you've had five. And Ernest Johns seven and a half. You're
happy with him as your mate?'

'I am. Always. For as long as he's happy with me. Though
he might have thought to be going as master himself.'

'Not Johns. I know him. He'll run out his days as mate, and
be glad to. Specially under a Torrance. But I could not ask him
now to go with less than ten shares, and I would not. Ten shares
it is for him.'

'Good. He's well worth it.'

'For you there'll be your father's ten plus your five, and five
more in addition. Twenty in all to you and ten to Ernest Johns.
With the men's thirty it'll be a deep cut for the firm, but I
think it's worth it.' His hand settled on Torrance's shoulder.
'I want to keep you, Robert, and keep you happy – for more
reasons than the fat you'll bring us. If it's not enough –'

'More than enough.' Torrance shifted impatiently. 'More
than I'd have thought to ask for. It was never a question of
sharing –'

'I know.' Bracebridge risked a chuckle. 'We'll say the extra
five are for Maura's son, if and when the young rascal decides
to arrive. Is it not high time you two were thinking of that?'

Torrance looked up then, but his eyes were vague and cold
under the slight, forced grin. The old man's chuckle died. 'Well,
well –' he gathered himself with an attempt at hearty briskness,
'are we all squared away?'

'Aye, sir.' Torrance gulped down the last drops of the sherry
and stood up. Twenty shares for a captain – it was more than the
firm itself would clear from the voyage. It told of his worth to
Bracebridge, and it told, too, of the current of talk that had run
about the port. Many a man had been here with it, and the owner
had listened to all of them, thinking of his business. The kindly
man had listened, thinking of Maura. Torrance could imagine
the sound of the voices here, guess at the words spoken under

the lamp-glow in the quiet of this room. He looked about him.

The decanter gleamed on the carved silver of the tray, and the heavy old-rose drapes were drawn across the wide window that looked down on the harbour. A log fell in the fireplace, and new light flickered on the walls. Darkness and spattering rain were shut away. The bookshelves climbed to the ceiling and the ranks of the leather bindings marched along them, untidily here and there, with the gaps in the ranks that indicated use. The globe stood on the wide mahogany desk with the files and ledgers behind it, and the dials of the huge iron safe winked handy to the desk chair. The dusky portraits in their ornate gold frames hung heavy and remindful, just above the fire-glow. Bracebridges of the past, Bracebridges who had sent his father and his grandfather and his great-grandfather before him out to the seas, north to the ice. The furniture was old and English, brought here by great old sailing ships that were forgotten hulks now. It gleamed with polish, it smelt of citron oil, it had been rubbed smooth by the hands of generations of chattering maids. On the outside, as you came up the muddy drive, the frame walls were as bleak and grey as the side of a warehouse, bare of paint, for there was no paint that could stand against the driving salt of the nor'easters. It made the change more breathless when the door opened on the gleaming hall and you stepped out of your squelching sea-boots and entered in your stockinged feet, always a little hushed, a little humbled, on this richness the sea had given.

Twenty shares; yes, the Bracebridges were fair and always had been. No Torrance had ever complained of them or ever had cause to. It was only now, in this moment, looking about this room, that the new thought came with a crawling, welling venom he could not understand. This was a Bracebridge here, this was a possessor. He was a Torrance and would always be, always the lesser man. What did he have to resent? What did the thought mean? He shook his head with a queer, dim gesture that the other man noticed with quizzical concern. He felt the glance and looked up, but it had slipped away. Bracebridge was sipping his wine, the worst of his worries over.

For a moment his eyes rested on the white head, measuring

14

the gulf that divided this man from himself, the gulf he had never wished to cross before. He did not wish it now, he envied Bracebridge nothing. The speech was not his speech, the life was not his life, the world of the great house, the desk, the globe, the marching books was not his world. What did it mean to him, then – why should it mean anything – that he was walled away from it? The question framed itself, answered itself. It grew from the long day, the long year, sweeping him round like a ship's bow in a swell, answering the relentless rudder. It fixed him on the other thought. That other gulf, wider and deeper still, dividing the boy Tim Mahan from the boy Robbie Torrance, the bastard brat of Dogstown from the son of many captains. It yawned before him now, seen for the first time clearly. The first time? He shook his head again. It had run between them all the days of their lives, shaping their lives.

He was back for an instant with the boy Tim, back on the rocky schoolground. He could feel that feeling never quite laid by as they booted a ball or roughed with the other lads. The possessor, he was the possessor then, and the lad never far from his side the hungering one. The patched, the fish-smelling, dirty, beautiful boy, aimless and silent and content with nearness. The voice came back, mingled with wave-wash, gull-cries; the brown, bare feet were padding the rocky shore, sinking in sandy slopes, scratched with the briars of wind-blown summer roses. He saw the boy bent over the briars again, stooping with casual care to pluck a rose, nestling it into his pocket and turning away, something unreadable hidden in his eyes. Always the other thing had been there too, haunting those eyes. That longing to be like, that sense of the gulf; it had reached across the gulf to the boy Robbie. He had felt it and refused to feel it, he had known it and not known it. He had been drawn by it and had scorned it in the pitiless way of boys. Boys – they were boys no longer. Let it go.

Bracebridge was on his feet and speaking again. Torrance came out of his thoughts, guiltily, and made a move toward the door.

'Robert,' – it was hard for the older man to get the words out – 'I've not spoken of your father.'

15

'No.' Torrance was gruff and short. There was no time for that now, and no use.

'What could I say that would help? You know what I felt for Lije Torrance.'

'Aye, sir. I do.'

'As for the rest of the talk – well, I've heard it, and I can guess what's in your mind. Lije didn't go over the side just for nothing. And if Mahan was on the ice that night – up to his old tricks –'

'There's no proving it.' Torrance was gruff still, anxious to be gone now. 'And there were no pelts missing nor any of the flags touched. So it's best kept to myself, whatever I think.'

'Aye – aye, I suppose it is.' Bracebridge drew a breath. 'Did it have anything to do with your notion to stay home this year?'

Torrance shrugged, warmed a little in spite of himself. Bracebridge too, then, was thinking of more than shares and money. He liked him the better for it. 'When a captain's in the ice,' he said, keeping his eyes on the cap in his hands, 'his business is his ship and his men. If there's anything else on his mind, it's too much.'

Bracebridge nodded. 'I thought that's the way you'd be thinking of it. I've no fear of what you'll do, Robert.'

'And you've no control over *Kestrel*.'

'Surely, man, he'll be keeping well off from you this year?'

'Will he?'

Bracebridge turned away from the hard stare, fretfully. 'I don't know what those damned Playfairs are thinking of! There's no other owner in the island would have anything to do with Mahan. If I'd my way he'd never take a ship from this port – or any port.'

Torrance shrugged. 'He brings back the fat – that's what they're thinking of. And he's a good seaman – as good as you'll find anywhere.'

Bracebridge drew a long breath and stood for a moment twiddling the globe on the desk. 'Yes, he's a good seaman – thanks to Lije Torrance. I made no complaint about it in the old days and I'll not say your father was wrong, Robert, but it was strange to me that he'd ever ship a lad like Tim Mahan –

16

or ever let the two of you grow so thick together.'

'Strange?' The word came out so sharply that Bracebridge stiffened. Torrance could feel himself bristling. That dim, buried, half-understood resentment was rising nearer to the surface. 'What's strange about it, sir? We'd been thick enough since school-days – and why not? We were lads of an age – he'd the same wants as I had – and less to satisfy 'em.' He stopped for a moment, surprised that he had said as much, and then the very room with its mellow warmth and comfort drove him to more. The day itself, with its hours in the twisting lanes and its restless swarm of memories, pushed him on. 'Up here on the hill ye don't get the stink of the streets he came from – Lazybank and Pokeham Path – Dogstown and Maggoty Cove – where ye walk on fish heads and fish guts and the drunks lie in the road with the dogs and garbage, where the roofs sag with the wet, and the doors hang on one hinge, and the whores squawk from the windows –'

'And the Portugees come when the fishing fleet's in.' Bracebridge was puzzled by his manner but was hardening at the tone. 'I know a bit of all that, Robert – more than you think. It was a Portuguese sailor that fathered Tim – not that drunken blackguard Kevin Mahan.'

Torrance shrugged impatiently, still with the nameless anger. 'All the town knew that – the lads in school knew it.'

'So did Kevin Mahan know it,' Bracebridge said quietly. 'But he kept the woman by him and he kept the boy – if you could call it keeping – for twelve years. And then one day the Portugee came back – maybe he'd been coming back every year, for all I know. But this time Kevin was waiting.'

He paused a moment, his eyes darkening with a memory, his lips hardening. Torrance felt anger go and panic come as he looked at the kindly, serious face, always so carefully shaved by expensive valets. The chill of twenty years before walked the length of his spine, stirred in the nape of his neck. No – no – stop him! The cry rose in his mind, thin and shrill as a boy's. I will not see it again! I will not hear it! But Bracebridge went on.

'I was called to the place next day – I was one of the

17

magistrates then. And I'd my first and last good look at Kevin Mahan – and at what was left of his woman. I did not want a second, I can tell you that.' He drew a breath and turned with a gesture of disgust, waving it all away. 'I know enough about Dogstown, Robert, and the scum that's bred there, but –' He stopped short, put a hand to Torrance's arm. 'Robert! What is it, lad? What's the matter?'

Torrance shook off the hand and made for the study doorway. He found his way through the hall with Bracebridge following. His boots stood in a damp circle on the mat, and he stepped into them and wrenched the house door open. But he could not make himself go, not yet. His voice seemed a stranger's voice as he swung round, coming from a stranger's throat, against his will. 'You've not said a word about the boy.'

'What?' Bracebridge looked at him blankly.

'The twelve-year-old with the patched-up coat and the leaky boots – and the eyes that didn't see you and the scream he couldn't stop.' He gathered himself, turned for the doorway, and once more turned back, still with a savage bitterness in that stranger's voice. 'But then, why should you? What was a lad like that to the likes of you?'

He was down the drive and onto the path for Water Street when he heard the step behind him. The house door had swung to with a great crash as he let it go, helped by a rough nor'easter. It had shut off the startled eyes in the ruddy face, the gleaming warmth of the hall. In the wet black of the windy night with the flat, pale taste of the sherry still on his tongue, his ears rang to the thin, shrill cry of a boy. The scream came back across the stretch of the years, the stench of the slimy street was rank about him. The cracked door opened in the sweating wall. He could see the face of the boy, the eyes that died in the boy. He could smell the Dogstown smell of the ragged coat; the cameo carving of the face was there, its olive pallor drained to a bloodless grey. And now it was the quick, light step familiar as a voice, and then the voice itself.

'Robbie –?'

There was the old lilt in it, and the old mockery. He turned, with sagging muscles drawing taut. The day's weariness ached

18

in his legs, the day's thoughts were still churning in his head, but the lies of the day were done with. Whatever he had said to Johns, whatever he had told himself, this was what he had wanted. And it was no chance meeting. He had been watched for, waited for. The wandering laugh came out of the rainy gloom, and then the tall shape. 'I knew it was you, lad. I'd know that step in hell.'

'And I'd know yours.' Torrance waited while the rain drummed in the puddles and the sweat ran in his boots. He had not seen Mahan for a year nor forgotten him for a waking hour. The cat's grace and the cat's unwinking eyes. The smile that came from nothing. The face grew on the dark and it was all there, that reckless, ravaged beauty with the stamp of the Portugee. The cap sat back on his head as it always did, the lock of black hair straying from beneath the peak. The steel of the gaff point winked. Always the gaff in hand wherever he walked. 'You deal with me,' it said, 'and you deal with the gaff.'

'Well, Robbie?'

The lilt was softer, but the gaff was ready in his hand. Torrance could see the knuckles white on the shaft. His own hands worked at his sides. Here, then, here in this windy darkness it could come. It must come. And yet he made no move, and the gaff came down. Mahan was beside him, turning into the path. The wet boots sucked in icy mud again. Again, as on a thousand times before, they walked along together.

H E could not remember a time when there had not been Tim Mahan. The memories paced along with the squish of sea-boots. They beat with the rain and tossed in the wind like gulls. The voice at his side spoke through them.

'It's a hard day you've given yourself this day, Robbie. With no luck at the end of it – no luck at all.'

'I did not expect much.'

'Ye did not expect any.' The lilting laugh came softly. 'Or even want it. But still you went round with your questions – ship to ship, pub to pub – fishing for what? A lad of my last year's crew, maybe? – with a big mouth and bad dreams? Why did ye want him, Robbie? What did ye hope to find?'

The mockery was more insistent. He would go on with it till he was answered. Torrance stopped and turned on him. 'D'ye need it in words? All right. My father was not alone on the ice last year. He did not drown – he was not blown off on a pan to open water – he was killed by someone else who was out there with him.'

'D'ye say so, now?' The voice was gentle, solicitous. 'It's a hard saying, Robbie. And ye hoped to find the proof of it round the port?'

'You were lying a half-mile off from us, and the port knows your ways. If there'd been one man who had seen you step to the ice – just one – you'd not be sailing tomorrow or ever again. You'd be looking out from behind the bars of a cell, with a rope at the end of your wait!'

It was bluster and fake, and he knew it. The fatuous imagining died as it was born, and the soft laugh came again, utterly knowing. 'I thought that's what you might be telling

21

yourself, though I doubt you ever believed it. So it was all to be work for the lawmen, was it? – someone else's hands? That's not the way it'll be, Robbie – ye know better. And it's not the way you want it. Were ye not hoping, as ye bustled about all day, that you'd come on me face to face? Well, you have. I'm here now.

'I'll ask you one thing.' Torrance bent in on him with harsh, evasive intensity. 'Why? Will you tell me *why* you did it?'

'Did what, man?' The tone was bland and maddening, wicked and amused. 'Ye've stirred yourself up with all these wild, bad thoughts. There's no soothing ye – ye'll have to live with 'em.'

'All right.' Torrance turned from him grimly and started on. 'That'll be the end of the asking.'

'And good riddance to it. Ye'd not make much of a lawyer.' They paced for a while in silence, and the voice was easy and casual when it came again. 'So you've been having a last word with His Nibs on the hill. I've been with my owner too. Just come from him when I met you, with his good liquor in my belly and my backside warm from his fire. Though of course he's no great rajah like the Bracebridges. Their kind won't have me.'

The chuckle came but the voice was no longer casual. There was the familiar quickening of the breath, the edge of wildness. 'Ah, lad,' – the sigh was playful but there were fires forcing it up – 'it's a fine thing to have a great house and a dozen ships of your own, and fatten on the backs of a thousand men. D'ye never think of it?'

'No.' Torrance knew what was coming. He could feel the old cold crawling in his scalp.

'Nor of how it'd be to strip him of it all?' The voice was rising, wandering and light again. 'Aye, Robbie – strip him bare to the white silk breeks and the skin, and have the lot to yourself. D'ye never think of that?'

'Give over your damned nonsense. I've heard it all before. We've other things to talk of, if it's talk you want.'

'Many things, Robbie – many things. But I think of His Nibs sometimes, and old Playfair, and the rest of the big ones

22

riding the crest of the hill – and of how it'd be to turn 'em out in the wet – pull down the houses and sink the ships – and start 'em again all even, two hands to a man. Two hands to a man, Robbie, and the world for the grabbing again, and the scraps and muck to the hindmost. Ah now,' – the step was sure on the slippery, muddy slope, quick and sure as always, but the words were breathless and shaken – 'there's a thought to live with!'

'Will ye give it over or get the hell to your ship!' Torrance turned on him again with fierce impatience. 'Ye stayed close enough aboard of her when I was round the jetties today. What d'ye want of me now?'

'Of you? Ah.' The voice steadied a moment. He felt the eyes on him, still alight in the dark. 'That's been the question, Robbie, for a long, long time. All those questions stewing about in your head, and they're all one. What do I want of you? What do I need to rid myself of the stink – to unmake the Dogstown bastard?' The laugh broke shrill and keen, not for Torrance alone; it was never for Torrance alone in these moods. He shrilled at the night and the world. 'I'd be needing all you've got – all you are! All that all of 'em have – and never enough still!'

'You've grown worse in the year, not better.' Torrance studied him with cold quiet. Over everything, in spite of everything, the old, numb ache of pity was flowing back.

Mahan quieted with him, sensing the change, resenting it. His voice came low and surly. 'Aye, look if you like, and think your thoughts. They're the half of my own, anyway, and no help for it. You've been too near to me, Robbie – too near.'

'And not once – never from my father nor me – have you had a thing but good.'

'Good!' The laugh keened up again, harsher. 'Aye – the scraps and parings – the bones tossed to the dog. Four years shipmates with the good and godly Torrances, and then the boot at the end of it and the march down the gangway. Do I thank old Lije for that?'

'And ye did not kill him for that. It's twelve years since he sent you off from the ship.'

'Aye, it is. And you're talking of killing again.'

23

'Because, God damn you, I –' Torrance broke off, and turned away again. There would be no answer but that soft, mad laugh. He did not need an answer, he hardly wished for it. His father tossed in the sea of the other thoughts, the other faces crowded over that face. The boots splashed beside him, the rain drummed on his shoulders, and the cry of the boy came back. The boy Tim no longer – this was the Jinker now – trailing the sullen name from ship to ship. The feel of evil walked with him. It walked here, but still the boy walked too. The memories would not go. Aching and clinging, never to be shaken off, they were crowding in again, the days on the rocky schoolground, the truant days on the cliffs, the days of the bird's-nest robbing, and the blue-mouthed days of the berries, the days when the squid came in and the capelin ran. Sweating in summer sunlight, soaked in the winters' sleets, blown in the winds, the days of the boys were back.

It was a queer friendship, even for that rough, storm-rattled little barracks of a schoolhouse, set on its stony acre. McDonough, the teacher, was curious and disapproving. Other lads, fidgeting at the much-carved, ink-spattered desks, with their eyes on the windows and their thoughts on the water outside, were often piqued and derisive. Why the rag-bag from Dogstown chose to be here at school when no one made him come seemed mystery enough. It was stranger still that the son of Elijah Torrance, one of the great ones in this community, should tolerate his companionship at all. Still it went on and grew in the way of boys, tacit and unexplained. Neither one questioned it or ever thought to comment on it. They came together in the schoolyard and the schoolyard remained their centre, opening out, as naturally as the seasons, to the shore and the water and the ramblings over the cliffs. Summer evenings and winter afternoons, often on days when they should have been in class, they found themselves on the hills, or roaming the docks, or climbing about on ships, or talking of ships. It was almost all that Torrance could remember of the way of their meetings.

When the day's business was ended they parted as casually as young Indians, each for his own world. There was no

24

thought of bringing this murky scion of Dogstown to the spotless home of the Torrances, even while Robert's mother was alive. It was even more unthinkable after she was gone, for a boy who lived herded about and harried by a succession of bustling aunts. Elijah Torrance, for a year or so after the death of a young wife, was a man dazed by his own hurt. If he knew of the boy's companion he said nothing. If McDonough spoke to him of it, it had no effect. Nor did the jibes of the other lads at school do anything to break the friendship. The boys simply found, when they jeered at the torn pants or the Dogstown smell of one, that two pairs of fists came at them.

They were each twelve on the grey September afternoon when they ducked away from the schoolyard. Tim had arrived with a sticky bag of sweets and was offering it with an air of excited mystery. Something in his manner seemed to encourage truancy, though it was a dismal enough day. When the school bell went, Robert simply turned his back, and Tim turned with him. A malevolent little wind breathing in short, uncertain gusts wafted them down toward the water. Wandering along the quays, eyeing the tied-up vessels, they ate the last of the sweets. They came on the empty dory with its line around a post. Grogan's dory; he'd be off for a drink somewhere, and probably for half a dozen. In five minutes, with hardly a word exchanged, they were putting out across waters already a little oily under the nagging wind.

It was all familiar mischief, with no thought but to get out to the near rocks and drop a jigger or a codline till a roar summoned them back. But they were hardly abreast of the rocks when the white water churning along their windward side and the darkening shadow in their lee warned them, as they should have been warned an hour before, of weather coming. It was Robert who swung the boat round and Tim who sat as always, speculative and obedient, waiting for what the other would do. Yet it was Tim, when the instant came, who moved with the swift, rippling sureness that would grow to be the mark of the man.

At one moment each was pulling at an oar twice the thickness of his arm, wrenched and tossed by the swelling force of

25

the sea. At the next an oar was gone, Robert's oar, and he was over the side after it, whether in a deliberate dive or simply a reckless tumble he could never afterward recall. All that remained of the moment, clear and sure, was the terror of cresting froth and battering waves.

It still seemed impossible that one boy with one oar could swing the boat so quickly to make a lee for the swimmer. Or that, still holding the oar, he could reach over to lock hands with the other and haul him inboard. Yet it was done, so quickly that terror passed almost before it came. Soaked and shivering, laughing and gulping air, Robert lay sprawled on a thwart for perhaps five minutes. Then they both tailed onto the single oar and brought the boat to the dock, tossing and lurching, wheeling in wide circles over the restless water. By the time they rode in stern-first, meeting the timbers of the quay with a mighty crash, the one worry left to them was the fear of Grogan's hand. But there was no sign of the red face, no shout for the lost oar. They climbed out, made the line fast, and scuttled away in safety over a deserted jetty.

They were Newfoundland lads with a hundred duckings behind them, bragged about and forgotten, a part of their growing up. This had been only another, yet one moment of panic, one false move, and Robert would have been done for, and he knew it. The other boy knew it. The new thing grew between them as they huddled against a wall, their teeth chattering, guilty, relieved, and giggling, soaked by the sea and the rain. The one who had always taken had given something back. The lad from Dogstown was the equal now, and felt it. For a single wordless moment they turned to each other, dripping and tousled, standing eye to eye, sensing the change. Then they both sneezed and the giggles began again.

'Ye'll be away home with me for a bit, and it's lucky it's this day.' Tim's words came with an odd peremptory authority, as the sneezing and giggling passed and the chill began to bite.

'To Dogstown?' Robert was dimly startled, not only by the words but by the new briskness of the tone.

'And why not?' The warmth and confidence persisted. 'If ye go back to your own place soaked and coughing and chattering, your da will know what you've been up to, and there'll be a whopping for you.'

'But I'm forbidden Dogstown – ye know that.' The words came out with a boy's innocence and cruelty, and Robert only measured them by the change in the other's face. Something was threatened, he did not know quite what; something would have to be recalled.

'Aye, so you are – I'd forgot. All right – go home and take your whaling.' Tim turned away. There was the vague, aimless reluctance of all the other partings and something more now, a new droop to the shoulders, a new surliness. 'Though there's none but you I'd ask – and we've a fire in the place today.'

'Wait.' Robert put out his hand. There was the chill of his dripping clothes and the thought of his father's face. There was a stirring of warmth at the hurt in the other's voice. There was a touch of curiosity; it was the first time Tim had mentioned his home or Robert had thought of it. He took an uneasy step, paused while the other watched him, and then they started together. 'It'll be all right for a bit – I'll come.'

'Very good of ye, *Mister* Torrance.' The surly hurt lingered for a minute, and then they both forgot it. They turned into the first of the lanes that climbed up from the water, turned into another that dipped down again, running always a little narrower, always a little more dank, by the back walls and the refuse dumps of warehouses. The squatters' shacks began to grow about them, with here and there the dirty lantern of a pub already lighted. As they came to another lane, barely a footpath now, litter clogged their steps, and dank old hovels leaned in on them, tumble-down and filthy. They circled the muddy hulk of a sleeping man, lying across their way. There were more drinking-shops, more huts patched with ancient, greying timber stolen from the docks or torn out of beached ships. There was a glimpse now and then of the harbour or the rocky shore as they followed the mazy windings up and down with the rain beating on them. There was the stink of rum and fish and excrement, the Dogstown smell, and the drifters who came to Dogstown lurched by them, loud with liquor, or sullen and parched for the lack of it. Evil old drabs

27

hanging out of windows or leaning half-naked in doorways bawled obscenities at them. A little sick from it all and a little frightened, Robert tried to keep pace as the other boy pushed on, familiar here and at home, with a new eagerness growing.

Some of the men who elbowed by in the mist seemed quieter and softer-voiced, with the clean smell of salt and the sea about them even in this place. There was a welcome colour and warmth in the bright scarves and the black hair, the glint of a gold earring, the flash of white teeth in smiling brown faces. Robert noted them dimly among the swarm of other sensations. Portugees of the fishing fleet, in for their day ashore. It came as regularly as the seasons, as sure as the cod or capelin, that cluster of well-trimmed vessels up from the south. Yet somehow the Portugees were adding to Tim's excitement.

'See?' He pointed them out with a little eager breath. 'Still ashore. Won't be leaving for their ships till near midnight. And Kevin's off up the coast to Harbour Grace. It'll be all right. It'll be fine.'

'Fine?' Robert looked at him blankly, chilled by the weight of his jacket and the cold ooze sucking at his boots.

'Ye'll see the place dressed up, and her in her best too. Ye'd not know her on the day the Portugee comes. There'll be cake and wine for the both of us.'

He was moving ahead, and Robert stepped out to keep up with him, glad to hurry through the reek and noise of the street. They were twisting down again now by another row of hovels, and suddenly there was a jarring stop. Three sleek rats went scuttling away from their feet. Tim had come up to a door, reached out to open it, and taken his hand from the latch. He was standing very still, listening. Over the sounds of the street came another sound from inside, a cry, and the sound again. 'No! No!' The boy's face went chalk-white, his words were hardly a breath as he swung round.

They started to run together and then turned, frozen to the mud they stood on. The door was opening slowly, edging out from the bottom, as though pushed by a child or a dog. For a moment the doorway gaped, dark and empty. Robert had a glimpse beyond it of rain dribbling down streaked walls, of

28

the leg of a splintered table lying up-ended, of a wine bottle lying beside it, and a smashed jar and a handful of wilted flowers that had tumbled out of it. Water from the flowers was mixed with wine from the bottle, and then he was aware of another spreading trickle growing from a shape at his feet. Slowly, horribly, passing with worm-like deliberateness at the level of his knees, the thing on all fours crawled by him through the opening. It was a man no longer a man, stark naked. The broken back sagged, blood gushed with the sobbing breath, there was no sight left in the eyes. As it inched past the boys, a red scarf and a pair of seaman's trousers trailed after it, ludicrous and obscene, clutched in hands that had closed on them by instinct. Robert saw the tangled mass of the black hair, the twisted olive face, the gold ring in the ear. Then it crawled on, blood spewing from the lungs with every gasp, and a rat nosed out behind it, following the glistening trail.

He did not know how long he stood looking, nor when he wrenched his eyes away. He did not run because he could not. He found himself in the doorway and then in the wrecked room, with the other boy beside him. He wanted to scream, to vomit, but he could only stand and look.

The naked woman was half kneeling on the floor, half sprawled across the bed. Kevin Mahan stood over her with his beltless pants sagging and the heavy belt in his hand, rising and coming down, rising and coming down. The iron buckle ate away the flesh of her back with every blow. The sounds that had been screams were choked now, coming in bubbling sobs. And over them, drowning them, guttural and rhythmic as the strokes of the belt, came the thick, rum-soaked litany of Kevin Mahan.

'Harbour Grace was it? Flowers and Portugee wine, was it? Not this time, me girl, not this time. Last year, the year before, and how many other years, but not this one. This time I'm square with the both of ye – I'll have me pay for it all!'

In Robert's mind the echoes of schoolyard talk came with the thud of the blows. Boys' words, the leers and nudgings of boys, tossed with the other thoughts of the afternoon, the thought of the boy Tim's face an hour before. He could not look

29

at that face, he could look at nothing but the strap in the hairy hand, the quivering, blood-splotched lattice of the woman's back. The buckle bit deep again, Mahan's arm rose again, and a strip of flesh lifted away from her body with a sound like wet cloth tearing. Her gasp seemed to fill the room for a moment, to stop time. Then, as she reared convulsively and fell sidewise to the floor, there was a scream from the boy Tim. It rose at the side of Robert, and went on. He turned at the sound, and it brought the end for him. In that cry, in the sight of the boy's wild eyes, there was more of naked horror than in all the rest. He screamed himself, and remembered nothing more.

How he got home that night he did not know. He did not know why he kept the truth from his father. He had played truant from school, he had stolen Grogan's dory, he had had a ducking in the harbour – all that came pouring out of him in an eager, breathless rush. Everything that might earn him a hiding, let him feel that strong hand, bring back the sting of love, the sheltering sureness. He wanted more than that, even in that first hour; anything that would let him share that other pain, give him a part in it, redeem that nameless agony and make it endurable. But his father did not beat him and soon gave over questioning him. He looked at the shaking boy with worried eyes and carried him off to bed. He sat by the bed through the troubled dreams of the night and watched for weeks afterward, searching for the heart of the trouble, groping with careful questions. He began vaguely to suspect a little of the truth, but there were no answers from the boy. The one ached to hear, the other to tell, but the words would not come. The two grew closer, somehow, round that silence, yet it changed both. The place of the son was larger in the father's life. The boy, wrenched loose from boyhood, was a man.

A port constable that night, stumbling along with his lantern in rainy darkness, looked in at the gaping door of the hovel to find Kevin Mahan. He lay dead drunk, sprawled across the blood-stained bed, while the woman shivered in a corner, half dead and half mad, the shreds of a dress clinging to her bare back. The body of the Portugee was found next morning by his boat at the water's edge, with one arm over the side. He had not been able to drag himself aboard. In a town with little law, even for those who were worth it, the perfunctory investigation ended there. The truth was well-enough known, and justice could hardly concern itself with a Portuguese whoremonger. Kevin Mahan had had his fill. He kept the woman by him as cook and bedmate, and she gave whatever he asked. There was no trouble left in her, with the lattice-work on her back and her eyes dead as the dust of the Portugee in the paupers' field.

Sometimes, tired of the sight of her, he would push her out to the streets to go about with the other drabs, finding beds where she could. But when he felt the need of her she would come back. He did not mind the harlotry and she often fetched him money. That much Torrance had gleaned of the year or so that ended with a tavern brawl and a knife in Kevin's back. The woman had sunk from sight in the stews of the port. No one had seen the boy, or thought of the boy, on the night the others were found. He never came back to the schoolyard. For a while Robert looked for him in his ramblings about the streets, and then gave over looking with a kind of guilty relief. The boy, gone from his sight, seemed gone from his memory too.

He was three years older, making his way through the stir of a busy dock, when he caught a glimpse of the sailor in from the south, shouldering a sea-bag down a schooner's gangway. Tall now, surer, with the swing of heaving decks in his quick, lithe walk. But still there was no mistaking him, and Robert stopped where he stood. He was bound for his father's ship that sunny morning, a lad with school behind him, a lad with a wound healed over, thinking of his own first berth. But he saw the dark head turn to him, the leap of light in the eyes, and he felt the wound reopen.

'Tim!'

'Robbie!'

They locked hands, slapped backs. Stevedores were cursing round them, and sailors elbowing by, but they stood face to face, conscious only of each other. In a moment more they were off for the jetty watchman, to stow the sea-bag with him. Then they were away, climbing the path to the hills, a bronzed lad in from the south and a lad bound outward, eager to hear of ships and the far-off ports. They sat on the high slopes while the sun warmed them, seeing the old sights, remembering the old days. They talked of everything and nothing through the hours of that afternoon, but not of the last day.

Why not? Why did all talk that neared the day of the dory, the day of the Portugee, of Kevin Mahan and the lash, seem to stop short, veer off? Robert did not know. Except that minute by minute the sense was surer; it was not to be talked of, not to this tall stranger. He could feel the oppression of that strangeness growing, and out of it the growth of the other thing. The light voice ran on, but the deep eyes burned into him, opening to some new need. The warmth and nearness suddenly became unbearable; he felt in those eyes a thing he could not name. He started up, still only half believing, and felt the arms close around him. The lips were brushing his cheek. He fought with tigerish panic and sick disgust and stood in a moment, freed. Almost as if the moment had not been. And yet it had. His arms were sore from that grasp, and the breath scraped in his chest. His spittle was glistening on the other's face; he could see the slow, cold emptying of the eyes. He came down the path alone with the form behind him, slumped on the darkening hill.

He lay awake that night seeing the bowed shoulders, the stricken face, sensing what had been done. The mind of the fifteen-year-old boy could hardly grasp it, yet he knew it was not to be borne, not to be lived with. He came to the dock next morning looking for Tim. He found a new stranger, a man with another silence locked behind him. The emptied eyes went straying away from his own, the light voice chilled him. Yet when he made his offer he was met with a grin and a shrug, and they turned for his father's ship. His father's face was stiff, and he could feel the stiffness of his own, as they came up the gangway asking to sail together. Let it be no – let it be no – even then in his depths he felt the cry for release. But his father studied the two and nodded, yes.

Four years together, the four years as shipmates, had come from that single nod, heavy, reluctant, and questioning. But Elijah Torrance's grave eyes often followed them about, often

32

hardening on Mahan. 'I do not know what it is,' he said quietly to Robert when the end of it all came, 'and I know you'd not tell me if you knew yourself. But I know this. He means no good to you or any man, and he will not sail with me again.'

There had been plenty of other berths for the sailor Mahan, and then it was Mahan the master. The master, always with the gaff in his hand and the mist of fear around him. The ship-drivers and the money-makers, the hard hands with men – there were enough of those in the port. They were a part of the luck of sailors, the life of the sea. But Mahan was another thing, with his fat cargoes, and his fast passages, and his log-loads heaped on the decks. The queer tales grew about him and followed him in from his voyages, and his crews left at the end of them. There was no luck in his ships, they said, for any man but Mahan. One by one, excepting always the Playfairs, the owners had turned their backs on him. A soiler of good ships' names, they told each other, a breaker of seamen, and a man possessed, a man with the devil's hunger.

All true, and all nothing. The twenty years went tumbling on in the wind. The sea-boots paced by Torrance, and the eyes were on him in the dark. He would not think of the rest, he could not trust himself now; he would break with more thinking. They would soon be down to Water Street where the path bent left and right. He turned to the other, gruffly. 'When we're in the ice keep off from me. Our business can wait.'

'Can it?' There was to be no relief yet; the voice still probed and jabbed. 'You've been giving me a bad name, Robbie, with all this tramping about the port – and a bad name with Maura, I've no doubt.'

'We'll not speak of Maura!'

The shout had laid him open. Mahan's laugh came shriller now, jeering and tempting. 'Now why not? Does she some-times speak of me, then? Ah Robbie, it was bad luck that you got ahead of me there. It might have been you for a cold bunk in a ship this night, and me for a warm home.'

'Will you close that mouth and be off! You've said enough.'

'A last warm night at home – what's wrong with envying you that? Ah lad –' the sigh was innocent, too innocent, the

33

pause was too long, 'the nights still come when I lie awake thinking of her. Does she sleep well herself?'

'You want it now and you'll have it now!' Torrance turned to lunge for him, and cursed himself as he moved. The gaff had hardly lifted, and the laugh was soft again, soft with the cat's content. His arms fell to his sides. He could not see the watchful eyes in the darkness, but he had no need of light. How many times before had he searched those eyes, aching for answers, hungering in gagged silence? The silence born that afternoon on the hill, locked with its double lock when the day ended. Never once, never in all the days since boyhood left, had they spoken of the other day in the Dogstown hut. He longed to speak of it now, and knew he could not. There were no words. Nothing could change again.

They straightened away from each other, and the wet glow of Water Street widened at the path's end. The sirens in the harbour rose nearer now, bickering and mournful. Mahan was shouldering his gaff, moving off. 'Easy does it, lad.' The chuckle came back softly. 'We'll keep for each other.'

'Wait!' Torrance took a quick step after him and the other turned. 'Get out of the port – off the island! Never show your face here again, and I'll not look for you!'

It was total surrender, the last shame of the day. Mahan stood for a moment eyeing him. 'As simple as that, Robbie? I'd not have thought it of you.'

He swung away with a laugh, and the darkness swallowed him. The squelch of the boots died out. There was only the other path now, and the other slope, and the waiting light in the window.

SHE had been Maura Bartlett, and she was now Maura Torrance, waiting for her man to come home. How many Torrance women had stood before her, watching at this window? Tired women and bustling women, women heavy with children, worn with the care of children, cherishing this place. It was as dear to her as it had been to any of them, yet it lay about her crowded with hostile shadows. She had brought them here; they had come on the day she came. They walked more greyly expectant, that was the only difference, since the day last year when the black-flagged ship came home.

Through the open doorway to the parlour the glow of lamplight hovered over polished woodwork. The smells of cooking lingered in the kitchen, hearty and warm. Outside, the face of the house, scarred by the salty winds, looked down on water. He had not feared wind or sea, the great-grandfather who had built this house, high on the cliff-side with its back to the town. She had heard much of him from Elijah Torrance and often thought of him now, that old, untroubled man she had never seen, watching for ships in day-time, talking of ships by lamplight. Now in the darkness, from this window where he had loved to stand, the unseen face of the cliff plunged down to the rocks. The leaden heave of the water coiled below. The sea sound came as always. Faintly, defiantly, the timbers creaked in the silence. The old house, like an old ship, breasted the moments of its hundred years, carrying her where? She had come to it as a bride, fearing the answer, and the fear was greater now.

Lije Torrance, the widower, had made her welcome, happy in his son's happiness. If he felt the shadows he had never

37

shown it; he had been the light that drove them back. He had stepped down with the easy kingliness of sunset and fulfilment to the third place in his house. She had loved him at first with the love stored up for a father who had never claimed it, and then wholly for himself. Yet when the ship came back last year in the March twilight and word ran up from the quay that he was gone, she had felt at first only a guilty relief. It was Elijah Torrance and not Robert, the lesser blow of the two. Perhaps it would be enough, she had thought, the price of peace. All that was over now. She knew better.

Robert had gone out this morning leaving his sea-gear strewn about the house. In other years it would have been aboard for a week. Yet the look in his eyes was enough to kill the small comfort of that thought. He would sail, he would have to sail, and that was the best she could hope for. The worst might come in the dingy streets of the town; she guessed his errand though he had told her nothing. In other years she would have spent her day getting his gear together, but she had not done it today. She had walked from room to room, window to window, chased by the shadows, fighting away the thoughts. As the drizzling twilight closed in, she had stood at the window looking down toward the town, hoping for a glimpse of the cap, the sight of the shoulders rounding the bend in the path. She moved to that window again, though she could see nothing; the last light was gone. The tide was coming in with a wash of surf; she would not hear footsteps. There was only the click of the latch to wait for now, telling her at least 'not yet'.

'Not yet' – the best she hoped for. It was a strange, chill thought among all the other thoughts, that the end seemed clearer than the beginning. No memory mattered now that went back beyond Tim Mahan. Yet she had been almost twenty before she had ever heard his name. Her thoughts fed and sickened on him, he swallowed her nights and days, yet for all she knew for herself or had learned from Robert he might have sprung like a genie out of a bottle, in full-formed malevolence. She knew it was not so. Something had grown before her that was not part of her. It was a part of Robert, the key to all the rest, and it locked him away from her as she from him. Yet he would not yield it up; perhaps he could not. Nor was she sure any longer that she dared to wish for it. With full knowledge must come the whole truth, and she doubted now that either had strength to face it.

For Maura Bartlett there were no memories of school-days in St. John's. She was born to the hill on the other side of the town. The Bartlett house stood up like the Bracebridge house, greyly aloof from the burly clamour of the port. But it did not know, in Maura's day, the sheen of prosperous content; she had come too late for that. There were dust and worry and debt in the study of Phineas Bartlett, and her memories of her father were the memories of a man going down, sharp-tongued, bitter, and absorbed. The fortune taken from the sea was being reclaimed by the sea, ebbing away in a dreary, relentless sequence of lost cargoes, luckless ships, and always more desperate ventures.

That was the theme of her childhood, with her mother's pride in counterpoint. No daughter of a Bartlett could be allowed to mingle with the rough lasses of the fishermen, or walk out with their sons over the scrubby hill-sides that sent back to the minister's door each fall their quota of tearful girls, no longer walking lightly, and of lads with the look in their eyes of dazed sheep. Maura was sixteen, in England, with three years of the school for ladies behind her, when the word came that closed the door to that world. The last of the notes had been called, the last of the mortgages foreclosed, and Phineas Bartlett had gone to his grave with nothing. The bleak old house remained by courtesy of Simon Bracebridge who had backed the last of the notes and would not take title. The mother sat on in the room she had always known, helpless and ailing. Maura came home to the woman and the house, and to what else she hardly knew.

For a year her mother watched a rainy window, huddled in rugs, unreconciled, unloving, unforgiving. The man who was gone had wasted all she cared for; she had no wish to join him. She had no care for his daughter and no desire to remain. When her eyes were closed at last, and the house wholly emptied, there was only a sense of relief. Then desperation came, and then Simon Bracebridge. She could have charity for as long as she liked, as much as she liked. Five generations of Bartletts had grown here, side by side with the Bracebridges. There were too many stiff old loyalties, too much pride of class, for Maura to be left forsaken. She would never go back to England, that was behind her. She would never leave the island; neither she nor Simon even considered that. She could live and go about, if she wished to do so, as one of the clan of the hill, the warm, closed circle. Simon would see to it with easy, sober munificence, and there would be no lack of a welcome for her in the friendly old drawing-rooms. Yet he knew, as she knew, that her days with the clan were over; she was no longer one of them if she had ever been. There could be the long death of clinging on like a limpet, or there could be the quick wrench of breaking. He was shrewd enough to guess what her choice would be, and he made it as easy as he could.

'You may not like the thought of it, Maura, and if so we'll say no more. For all I know it may be a scandalous new idea. But you've a bit of education, you write a fine hand, and it's the devil and all for me ever to find a secretary. I'm sick to death of wheezing old schoolmasters, and lads too stupid or lazy for a berth at sea. Why not a woman? There's a few would lift their eyes at it, but if you could bear the thought of the warehouse down there, and a desk in my office –'

Bear the thought! She looked around the faded Bartlett drawing-room and listened to old Aunt Em scuffling by outside, the septuagenarian maiden who had come from Sydney to live with her. It was almost the first thought she could bear since she came home. In a week she was at the desk struggling with the old-fashioned prolixities of Simon's correspondence, dazed by his strange sea-terms, her eyes aching from the long columns of figures in his ledgers, and her hands grubby with their dust. The clamour of the docks jarred her and yet excited her. The captains and mates trooping in and out of the office eyed her with stunned disapproval or open speculation, and all the world smelled of fish and molasses and sea-boots and sweat and wine and rum. She could feel the world of the hill closing off from her, even though she climbed the path each night to the Bartlett house and the lonely supper with her aunt. She felt it more surely on the rare occasions when she went from the bedroom lighted by a single candle to the drawing-rooms bathed in the glow of chandeliers. Her hosts felt it; she lived for a while between worlds. Then, incredibly, a kind of sureness and lightness began to grow in her. It was a poor enough life, perhaps, and always would be. But she had found it for herself and was living it.

Even now, almost ten years later, there was an odd little touch of pride in the thought that the sureness had come without the help of Robert Torrance. She had had something of her own to yield up to him, made with her own hands. Eighteen and a woman, a woman with a life of her own, she walked along the docks with him on that first day. She still thought of it as the first day and always would, even though she had seen him often enough before in Bracebridge's office and had known Torrances for as long as she could remember. But she had known them and thought of them in the way of the Bartletts and Bracebridges, the way of the hill. They were men of the ships, the captains and the hands; they came and went with the cargoes and were paid. One knew their names and faces, their good points and their bad points, as one knew the ways of vessels. One gave them orders and listened to their reports, and talked and laughed with them and sent them off, still strangers. Familiar as the cliffs, the harbour, and the sight of ships, known as well and as long, they were still of the other world. Without scorn or cruelty or even conscious teaching, one thought of them as creatures of the sea, mating and breeding apart.

Suddenly, on that day, the enormity of it all and the absurdity fell away from her. She wanted to laugh, cry out. The wind ripped along the quay, and she wanted to run with it, letting her hair fly, shouting the sudden joy. She was not shut in, she was free; she had lost nothing, she had gained everything. Life leaped and sang, free in the body of a woman, and a man walked by her side, the one man.

If he felt anything he did not show it. He was long enough and shy enough about that. She was still a Bartlett to him, it seemed, cased in and embalmed inviolate behind the polished rail of Simon Bracebridge's counter. It was a full year, agonizingly broken up by his weeks and months at sea, before he even climbed the hill with her and left her at the tumbledown magnificence of her gate. Then, abruptly, he changed. She did not know which of the signal hoists he read; she flaunted them all, shamelessly. But suddenly he was sure of himself and sure of her, and the walks on the hills began. He would swing along beside her slowing his pace politely, till from sheer pride she learned to step out as he did. She grew used to the seaman's silence born of the long night-watches, and it was soon an easy silence. It was broken more and more often by a great gush of talk, some rambling sailor's story of which she neither heard nor understood the half because she was listening only to the voice, waiting for the moments when the laugh would bubble up, rich and young.

She learned much that she had never known before about the taste and smell of weather and the moods of the shore by night, for they walked at all times. Whenever Robert was in port, as Bracebridge soon discovered, she raced through her work and was gone early from her desk. Aunt Em's signal was a lonely supper at home and a niece coming in to bed, wind-blown and very late. There was too little time for any coy manoeuvring or thought for the thoughts of the town. It watched them as it watched all courting couples, and this time with a new lift of the eyebrows. The eyes on the hill watched, too, and Simon Bracebridge was often quizzical, half inclined to protest. He thought better of it and so did old Aunt Em, though her protests would have been very faint at best. Her Bartlett hackles stirred a little at sea-jackets and sea-boots and the rough hands and the sound of the island speech. But she knew a man at sight though she had never known one in bed, and there was relief here from the thought that secretly haunted her of another old maid like herself, wizening over desks and ledgers.

Followed aloofly by watchers on the hill, eyed on the quays with ever-broadening grins, they went on to the second year. Neither Maura's house nor Elijah Torrance's house had yet seen much of them. Robert had an open ally now in Aunt Em, but he was still uncomfortable amid the cracked, decaying magnificence of bygone Bartletts, and at his own home he had no mother or sisters to show his girl to. He would not take her there alone when the house was empty; he had that much care for the proprieties. Lije Torrance was sometimes about and was soon welcoming enough, but his schooner was often out when Robert's was in, for they were each masters now who sailed together only on the sealing trips. The man and the girl lacked a fireside, and Maura would not subject him to the hospitality of the hill, even when a rare invitation came her way. Neither had any taste for the clatter of church sociables or square dances or picnics, and they soon tired of the dory rides that cemented commoner court-ships. So they were left with themselves and the island.

They explored the hundred paths that climbed up from the water and walked for miles, sometimes far into the night, among the rocks and sand of the shore. She came to know every view that the highlands around the harbour opened out. She stood with him, hand in hand, half blown from a dozen lofty perches, while the wind drove ragged clouds across the moon. She lay with her head on his shoulder while the low stars of summer seemed to walk on the still sea and the sea-fragrance met and married round them with the scent of the sagy shrubs, and the wild berries ripening, and the wild roses. Yet they did not once turn to each other for anything more than a kiss. From the first month she would have given him all he wanted, and been whole and sure in the giving. She was hungry and impatient for him, showing it in a thousand ways, yet she was still glad of his wait-ing. His hands were often hot, his body close against her, know-ledgeable and demanding. He was no boy and no virgin. Yet he would not take her till the banns were read, and the words spoken, and all made fast in form. She was safe, whether she wanted to be or not, and there was pride and sureness in that. Around them and between them, linking them and holding them apart, stood the old code of the seafarers, who might whore in every port but never their own, and who held their wives as sacred as their ships.

Whatever the whorings of the past, there were no more for him now; she was soon sure of that. Time after time he lifted out of the harbour, following the old routes to the old ports. The West Indies for salt, the West Indies for rum; always with fish to pay for them. Berbice, Bridgetown, San Fernando, Trinidad, Madeira, and Demerara, the Dragon's Mouth, and the Wind-wards, and the Leewards – they were all familiar names to her

43

now, and she was jealous of them all. He was months gone on the run to South America, into the doldrums and out of them, and up the river to Rosario, where the docks on the cliff hung high above the topmast and the great bales of hides came tumbling down in the chutes to splay out on the deck and slither across to the hatches. He told her of it all when he came home with the hides traded for molasses, and the kegs swinging from his hold. He carried Bracebridge fish to Spain and Greece and Portugal and came back with his cargoes of wines. The casks lay in the cellars under her feet as she sat at her Bracebridge desk, to go on to England, aged, in a year or two. There were the weeks of fishing on the Banks. Twice in their two years she knew the March day and the month of dread that followed when the ships put off for the ice. But he was her man through it all, hungering a little more, hurrying a little more as the lines dropped over the bollards and he set foot on the quay.

No talk of girls abroad and no evasive silences; that was enough for her. If there had been girls before her on the island they were well forgotten now, buried too deep in history to be exhumed. She listened with all her ears and heard nothing, as she certainly would if any of the girls had mattered. The joy and pride of possession were almost clear; they would have been wholly clear except for the one silence, the one blank space that seemed to gape in his life. Tim Mahan; the name seemed to cling around him. Wherever she heard of Robert, somehow, sooner or later, the talk veered round to the other. But it told nothing of the man, and Robert never mentioned him.

The two had been boyhood friends, she knew that. They had sailed for a while together and then parted. She could find no meaning in a parting of shipmates; it came to all sailors. Tim had gone wrong, the word came from the good; good men no longer sailed with him. Yet some men certainly sailed, for he was as much a commander of ships as Lije Torrance, more a commander, in one way, than Robert. In the ice the son shipped with his father and Ernest Johns; Mahan sailed as master. His ships were Playfair ships, always a little looked down on, for the Playfairs lived on the hill but were not of it. Newcomers and money-grabbers and rough-handed traders, they were New England stock, rather more kin to the first Bartletts and Bracebridges than to the latter-day aristocrats. Old Ebenezer Playfair, the claw-fisted, rheumatic patriarch of the family, still went to his counting-house and was still the impartial pirate to whom all methods and all men were good so long as they paid. Mahan ran his freights, and brought him cod from the Banks, and carried his wine and rum, and each March took over the black old *Kestrel* for the trip to the ice. And he made the trips pay; no one denied that.

There seemed a clue, perhaps, in the fact that they paid so well. Fat catches, clever cargoes, and deep log-loads were the mark of the great captains, and they meant more than money in the minds of seafarers. They were the measuring-stick of the eternal, boy-like rivalry that spiced the life. Wherever men measured other men, it seemed, the names of Mahan and Lije Torrance, or Mahan and Robert Torrance were set against each other. If it was that it was little enough, but she was soon sure there was more. Mahan was more than the shipmate who had fallen out with Robert and now tried to outreach him. He was more than a hard captain cut to the Playfair pattern. Simon Bracebridge grew tight-lipped and silent whenever she mentioned his name. The one time she raised it in the presence of Lije Torrance she was chilled by the look that crossed the old man's face. 'We don't see much of him here,' he said, closing the conversation like closing a hatch, 'or talk much of him.'

Few in the port saw much of him, it seemed. He was rarely in and kept to himself when he was. Curiosity in Maura sharpened to a touch of fear, yet she could not even catch a glimpse of him. A man would pass her desk and she would hear the mutter, 'Mahan's in'. Idlers on the quays would point to 'Mahan's ship', with no inclination, it seemed, to go nearer or speak more of it. Even on those two March days when the whole town blossomed gaudily and the sealing fleet went out with bells and jangle and commotion, there was only a mate to be seen on the deck of *Kestrel*. Mahan, the watchers told her, would be keeping to his cabin below, a man with none to wave to, bored with the cheerful racket. He was one of those seamen, they said – and they were common enough – who sulked and gloomed on a still

45

deck and only came alive when their ship did, answering the scend of the sea. Yet with it all, and always a little more surely, she was aware of his comings and goings. There was never a word from Robert, but a new silence came over him at the times when Mahan was in port, and there was trouble in his eyes. The two men saw each other once in a while, she took that for granted; but in what mood she could not even guess, for Robert's sombre quiet could have been grief, or anger, or fear. Then it would lighten away and she would know that Mahan was gone. Robert would be easier for a while, and hers again.

By the end of the second June her conquest of Elijah Torrance was complete. He had met her for a long time with an awkward, courtly, but formidable resistance. He was all too conscious of the hill she came from. He did not wish to see a Bartlett lowered, but he would not have Robert lessened. The daughters of the hill were to be bowed to, not reached for, and they had never seemed to him to be quite women. That was all changed now; she had put an end to it. She was more shameless and open with old Lije than she ever was with Robert. She was woman enough, she showed him, and no longer of the hill; she wanted to bed with his son. She shocked him, teased him, and sent him off sometimes into gusts of booming laughter. On the night he opened up on some of his own exploits in the ports of his far-going youth, and still more on the night when he threatened to turn her over his knee for some of her own speculations, she knew she had won him.

The rest followed quickly. With the word spoken in form and a date set, Robert went off to the Banks. Lije was there already, but he came back a week ahead of his son. The fishing could wait, he said. If there was to be marrying it would be done properly, and the announcement would come first. A man with no wife and one son was entitled to do things well, and it was a long time since there had been a party at the Torrance house. This would be one to remember. Aunts and assorted womenfolk would be summoned for the scrubbing and baking. Lije would see to the guest list. Robert would be no help and was better out of the way, and Maura would lend a hand with all the rest.

Everything marched to plan, duly and gaily, run by an

open-handed seaman who was accustomed to a taut ship. The July day came and darkened into a softly shimmering evening, one of those rare and lucky island nights when the chill of the north is gone and only the flowery breath of the Gulf Stream hangs in the air. The doors of the house stood open, and the wide, bare planks of the living-room, cleared for dancing, glimmered like tawny ice. She had been a little breathless at the wealth of old silver and the magnificence of the great punchbowl that Lije Torrance unearthed from a locked chest, grinning at her bewilderment. Grandfather's spoils, he said, not much used and the way of their getting better not talked of, but they would grace the supper table for this occasion. She had filled the rooms with wildflowers, waxed their well-waxed woodwork, beaten their worn carpets, and scrubbed their linoleum to a pristine newness. They glowed in the lamplight now, plain and square and warm, hung with stiff old daguerreotypes and cluttered with weird trophies that spoke of distant ports and many hundred home-comings. Her home now, or soon to be. She seemed at home already with that scurrying week behind her.

The groups and couples began to trickle in, all Torrance friends, stiff at first in silks, and crackling muslins, and dark, shoreside broadcloth, a little awkward with her. Yet the boom of seamen's laughter soon enlivened the room, and the eyes of the women warmed to her, quizzical, kind, and intimate. She felt herself accepted, and the warmth soon enveloped her. Robert, one day in from the Banks, moved about in a beaming daze, silly with happiness. She watched him from across the room, alight with his light. She was making her way toward him with Simon Bracebridge in tow, when suddenly his face changed. She saw that Lije Torrance was looking toward the door, suddenly stiff and angry, and she followed his eyes.

A man stood in the doorway, and she knew at once who he was. Afterward she assumed that he had been like the other guests, agleam from the hot bath and the fresh shave, prisoned in the shiny strangeness of a broadcloth coat and trousers. She could not remember; she could remember nothing but the impression of grace and lightness and the stab of warning. Instantly alert, instantly repelled in that moment, she could not take her eyes from the clean and perfect modulation of chin and mouth, nose and forehead under the cluster of black curls. She had never seen so beautiful a man.

All around her there was silence and a kind of shuffling back. No one seemed to move, and yet a lane lay open from the door to Robert Torrance. Mahan came down it, looking at no one else. 'Well, Robbie,' the voice was as soft as the olive skin under the sea burnish, 'I came in just today and I heard the news. I thought you'd not mind.'

'You're welcome, Tim.' Robert's face was as stiff as his father's, yet without anger. The words were somehow meant. She resented that, it separated her from him; once more there was that gap and blank between them. There was resentment everywhere around her, and distaste and withdrawal, and Mahan did nothing to dispel it. He came over to her with Robert gravely leading him, and his eyes settled on her and weighed her, almost, it seemed, without seeing her. He faced Lije Torrance with almost open defiance, and for a moment the goodness of the evening was wholly gone. But the old man roused himself with an effort she could feel, and his voice boomed out for all with a note of command in it. 'You all know Mahan,' he said, 'my son's friend. And now we'll get on with the dancing.'

Mahan did not dance, and she did not go near to urge him. As the strangeness passed, she felt only fury that the evening was spoiled for Robert and that Mahan knew it and wished it. He stood apart from the dancers, always alone, by the table where the white-rum punch gleamed in the silver bowl, potent and aromatic. It seemed to have lost its attraction for many in the room. They sipped what they had, carefully, and did not come for more. Mahan filled his glass once, sipped once, and then stood with the glass in his hand, motionless. She found herself, even in the midst of the dancing, watching that glass and that unmoving face. She found Robert watching her and looked quickly away, but it did not help. She looked again and was caught again. She was involved in spite of herself in a chilling, frightening game of cat and mouse that was all the worse for Mahan's indifference to it. There might have been no one in the room for him but one man. Wherever Robert moved, Mahan's eyes followed him, and Robert was aware of it. His face grew strained and angry, and tired, and somehow hopeless.

He seemed to shove it all away from him, with an effort that was visible and successful, when the music stopped and the signal came from his father. He moved briskly and smilingly through the dissolving sets of the dancers and came to take her hand. There was all she had ever seen, or dreamed of, or hoped for, in his eyes. Warmed by that touch and that look, as the circle of guests drew round her and Lije Torrance moved up to her other side, she had a moment of sheer, unclouded joy. Nothing mattered, her man was here, she was to marry him in a month; she was hearing the promise of it now. Then, as Lije finished his little speech and she turned to smile up at Robert through the flutter of applause and laughter, her eyes stopped midway, on the face of Tim Mahan. He did not see her at all, he was still looking at Robert and she was suddenly, terribly afraid. Yet there was in those eyes, unveiled and unaware for a single instant, something so sad, and desolate, and lonely, that her fear was tinged with pity.

The thought of that night hung over the following month and she would never be quite free of it; she knew that already. Yet excitement thinned it out little by little, and she was almost glad that the men were away again for three weeks on the Banks. It was a thing of much planning and not a little delicacy, this wedding of the daughter of a Bartlett who was now a penniless orphan. She would take no help from Simon Bracebridge; he would stand at the altar in place of her father and that was all. Lije Torrance, who would gladly have provided everything, would offer nothing out of respect for her pride. There was only Aunt Em to lean on, with a little out of her pension, and the wedding dress of Maura's mother, and a great deal of antiquated finery brought back from a hurried trip to Sydney. Bracebridge loudly bemoaned the loss of his secretary, but chased her home from her desk to begin her cutting and stitching. He would have to make do again, he said, with some pimple-faced wisp of a boy or some doddering relict of the schools, and a week or two more of her time would only spoil him; she had better be getting ready. The Torrance house was lively with the bustle of female

49

relatives and friends, and Robert came home three days before the day to a storm of demands and instructions. He seemed wholly himself again, a laughing, swearing, happily harried bridegroom, on the night before the wedding.

He was here at her house, he told her, to sit for a while in peace and avoid the confusion of his own. The women were driving him crazy. What did a man have to do, after all, but clean himself up, and dress himself up, and stand at the altar and promise away his life? The rest of it was diddle and daddle and better dispensed with. She agreed demurely, her head bent over her sewing, warm with the hunger she could feel in him as the last stitches went into the dress she would wear in the morning. Then, without looking up, she stiffened at the change in his voice.

Tim Mahan was in port too. Torrance had not thought he would be, but he was. He was a lad with a poor name and all that, and Robert knew that Maura did not look too kindly on him. *How* did he know? She had said nothing. What did he mean by it – if he did mean it? Why the long, awkward pause, the waiting, with his eyes on the top of her head? She was looking down at the dress, carefully. She almost looked up to ask some of the questions, to probe as she had never tried to probe before. But she held her head as it was, fought down the impulse. The needle went on, picking its way through the silk, while he resumed at last with that curious, pained, evasive effort. It was only that – well – they'd been friends of a sort, in and out, up and down, ever since boys, and he'd like Tim to see him married. He knew Tim would like it. Would it be all right with her?

It would not be all right. She was frightened by the violence with which the thought repelled her, by the almost physical revulsion she felt at the thought of those eyes watching her marriage to this man. Yet she nodded, still without looking up. Of course, if Robert wanted it. Why should it not be all right? She looked up then, quickly and intently, with deliberate invitation. This was the night of all nights when the last barriers should go down and the last blanks be filled. But he merely shrugged and accepted her words with a queer, quiet relief. Then he kissed her, holding her close and warm for a long moment, and took himself off.

50

She went to bed worried, and confused, and depressed. But when she woke in the morning with the sun streaming in at the window and a crisp breeze ruffling the harbour below, she was as light and sure and defiant as if the breeze had walked through her head, sweeping it clean. The world was hers and she would take it, for herself and her husband. She had no ambitions she knew of beyond that clean, broad bed in the Torrance house, but if Robert wanted it he would yet be an owner of fleets. She would see to it. And a father of many sons. She lay between the sheets for a while, luxuriating in the thoughts, smiling with them. Aunt Em brought her breakfast, a smile on her own craggy old face, and pushed her back to the sheets when she made a move to get out of them. It would be the last time, said Em, faintly riggish for once, that she would lie late and alone; she had better enjoy it. Em would be off to help the Torrance women. She would be back at eleven for the dressing and making ready, and sharp on twelve Simon Bracebridge would be at the door with his carriage.

The town clock a mile away struck eight. Four hours to wait. Maura finished her breakfast, propped on fragrant pillows with the sun warming her and the sea smell fresh at the windows. She heard the house door close as Em went out, and she lay there smiling still. Then, on a slow-gathering impulse, she threw off the covers and set her bare feet on the floor. She moved to the mirror and stood, for once, not seeing the crack that ran across the top, nor hearing the creak of the walls and the stealthy dribble of falling plaster that were the accompaniments to life in Phineas Bartlett's house. That death in life was ended, she was free of the last fetters; the more gloriously free because she had never thought of escape. She had wanted only the man and a share in the man's life, and they were four hours away. The body soon to be given to Robert Torrance throbbed and sang. With another impulse, born and grown of the first, she slipped out of the night-dress, moved closer to the mirror, and studied her white length, preening herself shamelessly. She had no cause to be smug, she told herself; she had not thought much of this virginity for the past two years, but it was wholly good now to have it still as her gift to the man she loved.

There was a sound at the window that was hardly a sound

at all, a breath, a stirring of the curtains. Tim Mahan stood in the room. He had come by the side of the house away from the road. The fence – the fence and the tree, she thought, wildly, blankly – she had often swung by them to the window herself. She had a swift and passing glimpse of the long-legged girl, the shreds of the tomboy memories danced before her, and then there was no more thought. Everything that had brought Mahan here was plain in his eyes.

There was no lust and no excitement. There was neither surprise nor hunger at the sight of her nakedness. The face was as beautiful as ever and even more in repose. It was the cold sureness that paralysed her in the one instant before his hand came over her mouth. Then she was tearing at him with her fingers and beating at him with her feet and knees, and abruptly helpless as he swept her from the floor to the bed. She sank back, her arms locked to her sides, crushed in the circle of his arms. He settled onto her without haste and without a word, letting his weight bear her down. She wrenched an arm free and clawed at his face, but he trapped it again, bent it under her. Her knees came up as he shifted and she pushed them into his middle, but the weight came down again. She was flat, helpless, his coat scraping her breasts, her knees separating, pushed apart by new weight. The hand over her mouth moved for a second, but the first gasp was choked back. The wad of the pillow-case came thrusting between her teeth, filling her mouth and throat. An arm above her was free now; she could feel the back of a hand groping over her nakedness. His middle lifted a little; she felt buttons and cloth go as the groping hand moved on, then the scrape of a belt.

There was the sudden warmth of flesh, the new pressure on breasts and navel, the hand more savagely urgent. Then there was the other warmth, warmth and wetness, the fierce lunge, the tearing stab of pain, and plunging, throbbing fire that seemed to go on through eternities and fill the world.

When it was over but he had not yet left her, he lay above her for a moment, his eyes looking into hers. His hand pulled the cloth from her mouth. The face was utterly cold, the voice was cold; even his breathing came steady and even. 'Scream now if you like,' he said. 'They'll find us so.'

He waited, meaning it, but she could make no sound. In another minute her body was free and she rolled away from him to bury her face in the bed. When she could look at him, he stood before her, buttoned and trim again, dressed for the wedding. His eyes travelled over her face and over her body, possessing them again, contemptuously. For a moment of utter silence their eyes locked. Then he turned for the window. 'All right,' he said, 'go to him if you want to.'

She lay where he left her as the town clock struck the quarter and then the half. She did not hear it marking off the first hour of bewildered agony and despair. Yet when the long strokes came again, she was listening to them. Her mind had cleared. She knew what she had seen in those eyes, the first night and this morning. She knew what she had feared and what she was going to do. Ten strokes, the clock was striking ten. She got up from the bed, took the blood-stained sheet to the monstrous old fireplace in the laundry cellar below, and burnt it. Em would ask for it, Em would be utterly mystified, but no lie could be as incredible to her as the truth. When the old woman came home, Maura was standing by the new-made bed, glowing and perfumed from the bath, dressed for the wedding. And so, in the white and filmy freshness, with the smile set on her face, she had gone to Robert Torrance.

A T the head of the path in the darkness the last big shoulder of rock loomed like a gateway. He came round it and drew a breath on the hill-top. A fresh gust caught him, beaded with stinging drops, but the square of light was ahead. As always for an instant, standing full in the wind, seeing the lighted window, he was pierced by a sudden thrust of meaningless joy. Chilled to the bone, wet with the rain, soggy with utter defeat, he felt her warmth about him. Then he was lifting the latch, the warmth gone.

He stamped his feet at the door of the little shed, and cleared his throat, and made a great business of climbing out of his boots and hanging up his wet jacket. The house door opened quickly and there was lamplight about him, but he kept his back turned. When he straightened in his stockinged feet to meet her eyes he was brusque and matter-of-fact, a man come home to supper. She would know that all was well, that the game went on; yet suddenly she was in his arms, her voice breaking.

'Oh Robert – I –'

He patted her shoulder gently, dropped an arm round her waist, and turned her into the room. He closed the door to the shed, summoning the man's laugh, ridiculing the woman's fears. 'Now then, I'm home – and all of me in one piece. And hungry as a wolf.'

She turned with a little happy flurry to the oven and the set table, seizing the mood and grateful for it. 'I won't answer for your supper – even if you'd come on time. I've spent the day at the windows. But I've kept it warm, at least –'

There was the stir of pots and pans for a while, and the brewis lifted its stout old fragrance from the stove, homely and reassuring. Her own fragrance stirred him as he stood like a man at mealtimes, always a little in the way, and she passed and repassed, smiling up at him. There was still the crispness, still the breath of cologne. Those clothes still slept in lavender, after the way of the hill. She had kept that and he was glad of it. He watched the quick, lithe body, the deft hands, the ripple and flow of light in the yellow hair. Free, like a girl's hair still; she had not come to the knot of the island women, and he was glad of that too. Nothing here he would change, nothing he doubted. They groped through mist and always groped apart, dreading the thing they looked for. Yet if it were found, laid bare, spoken of –

'Come now, Robert – it's ready.' The food smoked on the table and her hands fluttered over it, busy with the last dish. She looked up at him and the smile was there again, suddenly tearing his heart-strings. The blue eyes yearned for him, the blue eyes saw the way to him and begged for the strength from him to help her take it. And he had no strength to give. His hands fell from the chair-back and he turned away from the table.

'But you were hungry, you said!' The warmth of the home was gone. The homely protest died, false and mechanical. He moved with an impatient gesture, silencing it.

'Not now. In a bit, maybe.'

She forgot the food with him and came to him, her eyes changing now, searching and strangely resentful. It was that resentment, always with its hint of accusal, that stirred his anger and hardened it. If she had been defensive, guilty, pleading for herself, he might long since from sheer pity and love have let the thing walk into the open. She never had been. She had long since become the challenger. She had probed him to depths he did not know himself, could not lay open if he would. She was still probing. 'You've seen Mahan, then.'

He nodded. In seven years they had not mentioned the name a dozen times, yet it came now familiarly present as the sound of the sea outside. 'He'll be going north all right.'

He heard the slight breath, sensed the droop of her shoulders, though he would not look at her. 'Then you've found nothing,' she said, 'all this endless day.'

'Nothing to stop his going, if that's what you mean.' He turned on her. In spite of himself a note of harsh, hectoring jealousy was creeping into his voice. It was a new thing in this house; they had kept away from that. He saw her stiffening face and felt the warning, but the day had been too much. His pain poured out on her. 'Well? Why d'ye look like that? He's going to the ice, and I'm going. Is it not what you want?'

'Want!' She turned away from him and her voice broke. 'What does my wanting matter in all this? What can I do?'

The answer hovered on his tongue. She felt it in the silence and turned on him. Her eyes held him, transfixing him and tempting him, deliberately. 'Well?' she said at last, and he hardly knew her voice. 'If you have something to say, Robert, say it. If there is something you want to know, ask me.'

They had never been so close to the brink, never since the wedding night. He shrank back from it with a surly, fumbling evasiveness. 'What should there be that I'd want to know – that I don't know now? What's Mahan to you?'

She made no answer. It was not a question. He was taking refuge in a kind of schoolboy bluster and he was pitiful in retreat. 'From the first night you met him it was there – something – I'd not know what. It was there in the church with us, for all the blessings of the preacher and the frills of the wedding. If the time for plain talk's come, let's have it. Seven years now he's been the man in your mind – while I'm in your bed. Is it not so?'

She waited, steady and contemptuous, admitting everything and nothing. He fumbled on, wilder and weaker, wanting the words back even as they tumbled out. 'I've not blamed you and I've not mistrusted you – I've had no cause. There's no helping a thing like that, nor changing it – but there's no living with it for ever either, and –'

'Stop it!' She cut across his mouthings, furious and impatient, almost disappointed. 'Do you think you can make me believe you mean that? Mahan's talk – fed to you drop by drop! How many times have I seen him in seven years? How many words have we ever had together? You heard them all – you were there every time we've met – you were meant to hear them. And they were nothing – nothing at all. Is that not the truth, Robert – and all you want of the truth?'

He gave way before the newer, angrier challenge, though he caught its note of falseness. She was afraid too, as much afraid as he was. All that was left of their lives lay in their hands, fragile as crystal, tossed about like a ball. Yet still he could not stop. He shrugged sulkily away from her.

'All I say is, there'll have to be an end to it soon. And it may come in the ice.'

'Well?'

She still waited, steadily, challengingly. She knew it, then, and accepted it, perhaps welcomed it. In some dim way the thought was newly maddening. He turned back to her fiercely. 'It'll be done, then, won't it? – the choice'll be made for you. Whether it's to have him or be rid of him, I doubt if ye know yourself, but there'll be no more of this!' She seemed to be dissolving before him, sinking. He reached out a hand to catch her but his voice still went on. 'Oh I know – seven years married and true enough – and cold enough – but always with your thoughts straying. Never out of the mind, is he? – never out of the blood!'

He let her go, and she turned away from him and settled slowly into a chair. For a moment she put her face between her two hands. Then her hands went to her lap and she sat looking down at them. Twice he thought she was going to speak, and twice she caught back her words. When they came at last they were listless and defeated, almost idle. 'This is the sickness speaking in you – his sickness. Why do you spend your anger and your fear on me?'

'Fear!' He bristled like a man afraid, and knew it. She got up and came to him again.

'Do you remember the first day we walked on the quay? – or the two years after that? You could have had me for the taking and you knew it. Was I cold then? What changed me? The glimpse of another man – a month before our wedding?' She gave a broken little laugh, harsh and short, and her head leaned in against his chest. 'Oh Robert – Robert –'

His fingers caressed her shoulders and strayed to her hair. Over her bent head the cold crescent of a waxing moon looked in at him from the window. The night was clearing. 'There. Let be.' His voice was husky and gentle. 'We've said enough.'

58

'Enough!' She stiffened away from him with suddenly renewed anger. 'We've said nothing – as usual. And in an hour we'll go to bed as usual – to lie there with the thought of him between us. Every night – all my nights –' her voice broke again, 'I've lived them not with one man but with two!'

'Stop it, I say!' His own voice rose to a shout, but there was no stopping her. She was flinging his own words back at him like stones.

'Never out of the mind – never out of the blood – yes! But you speak for yourself more than you speak for me. What did I know of Tim Mahan till I knew you? What did I care? What do I know yet, but the one thing you will not see – or cannot bear to see?'

He felt his face stiff and his forehead damp with sweat. He had no thought now but to turn her aside, escape. Cold and hard and panicky, he went back to her earlier word. 'You spoke of fear. D'ye not think I've cause to be worried in the ice, with two hundred men on my hands?'

'Of course.' She looked up at him quietly and lowered her head again. She was not to be diverted. 'But we are not speaking of that, and well you know it.'

'What, then? I'm afraid for my own skin?'

'No.' She seemed to be lost in herself, hardly listening. 'Your father knew what it was – or I think he knew. I think he is gone because of it. Yes!' – she felt him stiffening away from her but there was no stopping – 'you will not say it, but I say it – Tim Mahan killed your father because he was a part of you – he possessed a part of you – and it was too much! As I am still too much.' She was very close to him now, her fingers plucking at the raw wool of his sweater. She searched for his eyes but he would not raise them to her. 'Too much, Robert – even this poor little that is left to us now. Everything must be Mahan's.'

'What's this now?' He forced himself to a blustering, shaken laugh. 'Are ye talking magic and devilry – like some old woman of the docks?'

'Believe that if you wish.' There was almost contempt in her tone. 'You know better.'

'They've fastened that badge of jinker onto him – and what

59

of it? There's never been a hard one knocking around the ports that didn't come by the name sooner or later.'

'I know.' Her eyes were steady and unyielding on his face. 'I'm enough of a Bartlett to know that. But it is not the same with this one. There is the devil in Tim Mahan, and madness and more than that. He is the one man in the world I could wish dead. Do you want to know why, Robert? Do you want me to tell you why?'

He shrugged away, a man impatient of a woman's folly. But it was refusal, clear and definite enough. She accepted it and her face closed with the finality of it, but she was not yet finished. 'I do not know what it is that ties you to him – you will not tell me – but I think you know. How can you not know, Robert?'

He was looking at his hands again. The hard, scrubbed knuckles stood out white on the brown skin. She waited, hardly hoping, and went on.

'You are not blind, and you are not a child. When have you seen a woman with Tim Mahan? What does he want of women? What did he ever want of me, except to be rid of me?'

He looked up slowly at that, but there was only a new stillness in him. They were nearer together than they had ever been, and he was still unreachable. She knew it for the first time now with utter sureness. They would go on, islanded in separate hells. She had built them with her silence; she had given Mahan the key. 'Scream now,' he had said with her nakedness between him and the bloody sheet, and his weight pressing her down. He had meant it, wanted it, and had not got it. She had not screamed; she had defeated him in that. Blindly, instinctively, she had made her bid for life, and she had gone on making it when her thoughts cleared. She would say nothing where nothing could now be changed. The forced and stolen body was inviolate and inviolable still, still Robert's. She would win this husband wholly to herself and in the winning blot out all the rest. She had not won. Nothing was blotted out. There was only the silence, and the wall she had built, and the key in the other hand.

Her husband's eyes were still searching her face. There was pleading and warning in them; she had said enough. Yet she was going on; she knew it. The words came idly, out of her own de-

60

spair. 'If you would tell me what it is – what he has been to you –'

There was no answer, and suddenly her voice was a scream. 'You will not be free of him as long as he lives! Do you even wish to be free? Those eyes of his cry out whenever you meet – and something in you answers!'

He gave to the last blow and then, abruptly and strangely, he seemed to be wholly relaxed. Yet he could not bear the house, the room, her presence a moment longer; she felt that. He started deliberately for the door to the shed. With his hand on the latch he turned, and his voice was as quiet as the sound of his stockinged feet. 'I could tell you the whole of it,' he said, 'and it would tell nothing. Can you believe that?'

'No.'

He nodded as though it were a confirmation, accepting it, unangered by her resentment. He opened the door to the shed, hauled on his boots and jacket, and took his cap from the hook. The words came almost formally as he turned with the cap in his hands. 'Ernest Johns could take the ship to the ice. If you wish it, I'll stay home this year.'

'And go on as we are now?' Her face closed and she turned away from him. This morning, an hour ago, she would have lighted up with joy and relief at the thought. They were beyond the hope of any respite now. A breath of the night air came, the door swung and latched, and when she turned again he was no longer in the house.

She lay the night through alone in the big bed, hearing his slow steps on the rocky ground outside pass and go on, stop, pass and go on again. Another night of seven years of nights, and this was the last of them now; if ever there were any others they would not be the same. Never another night like those they had known. She did not wish for them, she could hardly bear the thought of them, and yet the hunger for him burned like a still flame. Even now, as she lay listening to his steps, it came, devouring her anger, eating away fear and despair. There was a kind of torturing joy in it, a kind of hope; her body would not believe what her mind knew. It seemed a thing apart from her mind, this body; it always had in this bed. What had it told him

61

through these years, she asked herself, while she told nothing? In the wild, forced frenzy of the wedding night she had clung to him as to an anodyne, a death, clutching at forgetfulness, blotting out thought. And the leaping joy had surged in the spoiled body and been answered, answered with a fulness as though that noon had never been. Yet she had failed; she had failed on all the nights.

From the first moment of the first spent parting she had come to dread the other moments like it. The face on the pillow beside her with the moonlight playing over it had been the face she had seen in the church, heavy with bewildered trouble, the rejected thought gnawing at it. Mahan had been in that church, Mahan's eyes on both of them, and she had placed too much faith in her own numb composure. She had not known how well the man who loved her knew her and read her. She knew now, she had learned it in the long nights since he had found her not a virgin. The walks on the hills and the words on the hills had come back, haunting him; how could he help it? No man – there had been no other man – she had said it a dozen times, laughing at him, tempting him. It had been a light enough thing then, part of her giving, part of the all-knowing that she wished him to have. But it had been no lie. Suddenly it was, and suddenly the name of Mahan froze her and silenced her. How could she blame her husband that it froze all else?

The thoughts walked on, the weary, tattered procession, the memories of this bed. She stirred restlessly, wishing for the dawn. She had gone out from that church sure, justified, innocent; doing, she had told herself, the one thing that could be done. She had gone on beyond that wedding night, still sure, still justified. She and Robert had been lovers, they had been husband and wife, they had withheld nothing. And given nothing; it was there to give no longer, it was gone from each. They had known it for a long time, denied it for a long time before he came home with the word that Lije Torrance was gone. On that black night he had taken her with a passion she had never known before, and clung to her desperately long after, sobbing and wordless. But he had not found what he needed, fiercely as she had tried to give it to him; it had been the farewell. Together and alone for a year now they had lain side by side in the great bed, looking up into darkness. Sometimes in that darkness the one hand had reached out for the other and had found it and held it fast. The thread of trust still held but that had never been threatened; it changed nothing. They lay each in the solitude made deeper by the other. She had done him evil, though it was not her evil. She had spared him nothing. She had saved nothing.

Y E cleared Port o' Spain on the tenth of July. Ye ran down the coast to the Crawford Pitch Works and ye loaded up from the lake. And what then, Mahan? What was the trouble about? Will ye tell me what was done – what I can say?'

'What was done – or what ye can say? Now that'd be two questions you're asking me.'

Old Playfair wheezed angrily. Under the dim cabin lantern the veins and blotches in the dried-up skin of the face stood out black. The letter shook in the white claw of the hand. Dead white, fish-flesh soft, a hand for counting bank-notes, turning the pages of ledgers. There was always the spice, with him, of toying with an old spider, deadly and swift, but rattled and scared to strike. Yet there was no time for it now, no taste.

'Mahan! Are ye listening to me? I tell you I must have an answer!'

He was not listening. His thoughts were still above at the fork in the path, with the parting an hour ago. They were reaching on to the ice. The hot sun, the blue West Indian water, the stink of pitch – all that came with the old man and the letter – were a part of last summer's voyage, a part of all the voyages, left in the haze behind him. They were not worth the thinking of, they brought the throb to his temples; he could feel it beginning now.

The carriage had been waiting by the dock, empty, as he came down Water Street. He had seen the glow of the lamps ahead of him in the wet mist and had caught the scent of trouble. He had rowed out in his dory under the stern of *Jean Bright*, sedate and easy beside her Bracebridge quay while the ship of the Playfairs swung with the anchored herd. Old Ebenezer him-

65

self, with his two canes and his coachman, had been waiting on *Kestrel*'s deck, eyeing the crew dourly, knowing their worthlessness and counting the cost. But he had not come for that. He had waved Mahan to the companionway with the letter in his hand, and had struggled along ahead to be winched down by the coachman. Now the man was outside the cabin door and the letter was here between them. Mahan shrugged impatiently. 'I was up at the house not two hours ago. Ye could have had it out with me then.'

'I could not. It came to me after you left. Just in by packet. And it comes from the hand of the British Consul himself – it means what it says. "You are informed that from this date onward," ' – he was reading from the letter grimly – ' "there will be neither dock space nor clearance in the harbour of Port of Spain for any Playfair ship." '

'All over one fat black? – and a few tons of pitch?' Mahan laughed. 'It'll die down in a month.'

'Hark to me!' The old voice grated savagely. 'It'll not die – no more than the other stories. You're closing all the ports to me one by one. There's ruin in this, you fool!'

'So I'll not see Port o' Spain for a while, nor carry pitch to Boston. I can bear that well enough.' Mahan tossed his cap to catch its hook on the bulkhead and watched the dribble of wet forming beneath it. 'D'ye ever think what it's like, Playfair, getting those freights of yours?'

'I've made the run in my day. I know.' The old man gestured impatiently.

'Aye. And ye sit in your office now, or up in your big house, thinking of the lads that fetch your money in. Glad you're a lord apart, fattening up on the thin ones. Rum or wine, fish or fat, it all comes to the same, eh? And pitch. Aye, Crawford and Son of the pitch lake – you'd know of them, you're twin to them – with their docks, and lighters, and their big houses in the green trees by the shore, and their private hell behind 'em. Always the big ones' houses, anywhere ye go, and thatch and dung for the rest!'

The throb was hurting now, he could feel the flush in his face. Sun glare and water glare, the heat of the black-streaked sand, the smell of the squalid huts, it was all rising round him.

66

He could hear the groan of the carts, the pad of the splayed bare feet, the keen of the chant:

Ain't a-lookin' to de left,
Ain't a-lookin' to de right,
But a-walkin' in de middle of de road.
Keep a-walkin',
Keep a-walkin',
Keep a-walkin' in de middle of de road.

He could see the murky sheen of the great pool, welling amid the forest it had killed, lined by its skeleton trees, its tumbling thatched huts. Stinking of hell, more desolate than desolation. It had flowed down toward the sandy shore by day, hardening with the night cool, creeping with the sun again. Its stealthy progress had made him think of the ice. Bubbling black in the centre, warmed by the fires below. It had made him think of himself.

'Remember the lake, Playfair?' He roused himself from the thought, but could not leave it. 'Remember the hundred blacks that Crawford kept there, to scrabble the stuff out? Shovelling it into the carts, hauling it down to the lighters, filling those great grass baskets with their bare hands? Dawn to dark and back in the morning for more, with yesterday's hole gone. It's filled up in the night. Remember that?'

'Aye – aye – I've seen it.' Playfair waved it away, fretfully.

'With the sun beating on the lake and the black stuff giving it back, feeding heat from beneath. It's rock and glue and slime, and it's poison too. Ye never know where it'll give and suck ye down. It'll blister your bare skin wherever it touches, and you're smeared with it head to foot. You're working, a mass of blisters or a mass of grease, for a bed on mud, and a thatch over your head, and a scrap of meat on Sunday. Daylight to dark your life long – boy to man to the hole in the graveyard at last. With the boss man standing over you keeping the tally –'

'Ah.' Playfair stiffened. 'He was the one – ?'

'He was the one.' Mahan grinned at him briefly, idly. 'Inspector, they called him. Black too, but he could write, he could add figures. He lived in the littlest of the big houses – he kissed the white backsides. He'd a belly like a seal and a mouth like a cod, and the belly went up and down and the mouth in and out – both together – pouting. In and out, up and down, rotten with wind from the last meal, tasting the taste of the next. That was the god they had, Playfair – he was God there.'

'And he –' Playfair stopped, dreading to ask the question.

'Aye, he did.' Mahan laughed. 'It was a mere matter of profit and loss for the both of us. The pitch goes into the hold like coal, d'ye see, but it settles down like tar. Ye can't load full – it'd be too much weight too low – ye'd sail stiff. But ye *can* put in a 'tween-deck with an air space underneath – *after* ye've tallied your cargo.'

'After?'

'Aye, man – did ye never think of it in your day? It's new space – for unofficial cargo. Ye load a thousand baskets the last night, with a shilling apiece for the blacks and a pound or two for the inspector, and the rest free. But it went just a wee bit wrong, this time. He asked for twenty quid.'

'The inspector?'

'Aye, old fatguts. And he made the mistake of coming aboard to get it. He was standing by an open hatch – opening clear through the 'tween-deck, right to the stuff in the hold.'

'Mahan!' Playfair's voice was husky. 'For the price of a hundred tons of pitch ye'd –'

'It was two hundred by rights. The half went to me. And you were happy enough till ye got the letter. You knew all about it. Did ye not see by the manifests that we carried more to Boston than we tallied for at the pitch works? D'ye think pitch breeds? Ah no – ye steal what ye get in this world, if ye get anything.'

'But this was no mere black – this was a company inspector. They'll never rest now, man, till they get the truth of it!'

'Then tell 'em to look in Boston. If he's not been fished out he'll be somewhere down in the tar of a fresh-paved street. Will ye write that to the Consul?'

'God!' Playfair's wheeze was almost a shiver this time. 'You're getting too rich for my blood. Three years ago a dory with five men, set adrift on the Banks –'

'Lost in the fog, I tell you! How many times must I say it?'

'And what do you say of the lighter in Montevideo – that any man would believe?'

'Why, I've not said much at all.' The lilt was mild and amused. 'But you can, if you like. You can say the crew were drunk and they let her cargo shift – all but a little bit of it.'

'Aye. All but a little bit of it. You know where that cargo went, and so do I.'

'Well then – were ye not content with your share?'

'My share – aye. Ye've bled and cheated me along with the rest. I've not complained – I've kept my thoughts to myself. But there's some things come high – too high. You opened that lighter's sea-cocks and you sent her down with her crew, and they'll have your neck for it there if you ever go back.'

'It's my neck.'

'And it's my ships you sail. There'll not be a port left open to 'em if it goes on.'

Mahan eyed him quizzically. 'What's got into ye tonight, Playfair? Is it just the letter?'

'Is it not enough?' The old man fluttered the crumpled sheet defensively. 'How am I to answer it? What story can I give 'em? There's no help there from you. And on top of this there's the new talk in the port – the ships and streets are buzzing with it.'

'Ah.' Mahan was abruptly alert, carefully attentive now. 'There's nothing new about that. Except that Robbie's been stirring things up a bit. You knew it – you've ears everywhere. But you said nothing at the house.'

'What should I say? – with the start of the hunt tomorrow and this crew of rubbish aboard. Who'd take 'em, if not you?'

'If not me? Now it's a wounding thought you should even ask that question.' The lilt came briefly back. 'I'd thought we were a good pair, we two. Each for the other and both against the rest, and be damned to all the lot of 'em. But I've no need of your ship, Playfair, and no need of you. If you've any mind to be rid of me –'

'Now?' Playfair grunted fretfully. 'Ye choose your times well. But don't try me too far. You've made me money and I've kept you for it. It's the one reason, but –'

'The one?' Mahan leaned in on him, suddenly hard and dangerous. 'Are ye sure there's not two? How would you like the thought of Mahan against you – Mahan in his own ship – taking the fat, bidding away the cargoes, stealing the good runs out from under your nose? D'ye not think I could do it? D'ye not think I would?'

'As an owner?' Playfair studied him, almost openly daunted. 'You've no notion of what you're talking of. You've not enough for that.'

'Have I not? You'd be surprised what I've picked up here and there, and salted away safe. I'm not a man that throws his money about now, am I?'

'You're not a man that lives like a man at all.' The old voice was husky. 'And God knows what ye want. There's no money in blood, man. D'ye take joy in a killing?'

'Now who's talked of killing?' The voice was sliding into the lilt again. 'Mischances, maybe – they're always happening. The sea's a rough life, Playfair, and when a man's athwart of another –'

'You do take joy.' The old eyes were on him, steady and a little appalled. 'And the day your luck runs out it'll be the end of mine too.'

'Luck!' The lightness and mockery in the voice were gone. The laugh was a harsh bark. 'Eighty years on your shoulders, and ye walk with two canes, heaved about by a coachman. The breath scrapes in your throat, ye live on milk and pap, your bones ache the livelong night and day – and ye still talk of luck! Is it luck to live, you ruin – young or old?'

Playfair's bent shoulders hunched under the words. He turned slowly and clawed up his canes from the cabin table. He went to knock on the door to summon the coachman, then stopped, inched round, and pointed a cane at Mahan. 'There'll be no thieving of pelts in the ice this year, mind. None. I'm warning ye.'

'And who says there's been any thieving before?'

'If it was all that was said –' The raised cane fluttered down, waving it away. 'When have ye not come back with that talk behind you? But it's not all, and you know it's not. It's –' He hesitated again, then looked up directly, stiffening himself to the question.

'Will ye tell me what it is between you and the Torrances?'

'Between me and the Torrances?' The bland and maddening innocence was back again. 'Why, Robbie's my best friend – you could say my only friend. Would it surprise you to know that we walked down from Bracebridge's, just an hour ago?'

'Tonight?' Playfair's eyes widened in their bushy caverns. 'After all his searching round through the port today?'

'And why not? He was out to quiet a rumour. It's no secret, is it, that I was not the favourite seaman of Lije Torrance?'

'No.'

'But Robbie now – why, Robbie and I've not changed in twenty years. Schoolmates – shipmates – lads in different ships, masters of our own ships – we started off together and it's not changed us. I tell you, none of it's changed us!'

He was suddenly restless, irritable, conscious of the sodden weight of his rain-soaked jacket. He jerked its fastenings open, flung it on a bulkhead hook, swung round on Playfair, and turned away again. Changed – why should he talk of it to this old hulk? He knew his voice was changing, he could not help it. In a moment more he would be at his groping again, and he would not have it. Groping was done with now, long done.

Yet it was still there – that gap, that band of blackness. A day – two days – a week – stolen from a man's life. The days of Robbie and Tim, the days of the boys – they were all clear, all there. The rocky yard, the shore, the days on the hills – all clear as sunlight, never to be let go. All clear to where? – where ended? Suddenly – nothing. Darkness – the wet, black night – the schooner's deck. The shivering boy, mud-spattered, splashed with blood. Whose blood? What did it matter now? – there had been blood enough since. Yet how? Why? How was he there, the lost days black behind him? Not to be asked, not to be asked, that question. He could feel the throb in his temples, his breath was quickening. That soft, relentless pressure like a thumb – he thought of it always as a giant thumb – pressed at his forehead, pressing darkness in. Rocks in that darkness, danger, the pounding wash of waves on a lee shore. He clawed away from it

71

like an anchor dragging in sand. 'No change, I tell you – nothing – we've never changed.'

'Ye did not set off as shipmates.' Playfair was eyeing him curiously, aware of something. 'Ye told me once ye'd left Robbie in school.'

'Did I? Well, it was true enough. I shipped early. I'd three years at sea before he started.'

'Three years with Lije Torrance?'

'No, no!' He shook his head impatiently, anxious to end the talk. He moved about fretfully, searching for words to end it. They would not come. The schooner – that first schooner – he could not remember its name. Only the feel of the boots, heavy with shoreside mud, stumbling to the deck's heave. The sailors shouldering round him, the bunk's darkness – that other dark, restless with questions, stirring with its shapes. Faceless and eyeless, shapes of the sweating dreams, gone with the waking cry. Long gone. 'She was a trader, the first one – Nova Scotia vessel. In for a bit of fish and bound south. I shipped with her far as Cadiz and then I left her. I learned fast.'

'And when did ye ship with Torrance?' Playfair was still watching, still probing.

'When? When I came back – when I'd learned a bit of my trade. And what's it matter to ye anyway?' He was growing angry under those slitted eyes, angry and reckless. They were crowding back on him now, the times, the faces. He let them come, letting the silence lengthen. They were the best, the good ones, after all, those years of the learner braced on the washing decks. Once more the gusty mornings blew round the boy, blowing away the night-time fears of the bunk. The questionings lay stilled and settled, buried deep, stamped under by the march of the boisterous days. A lad's hands hardened with the running rope, curved to the shape of halyards, bled to the scrape of reefpoints. Sailors and sailors' ways, the ways of ships, he aped them, grasped at them, and drank them in. He lived in wide sea-light for the lift of landfalls, for shore days, pay-days, and the soon-spent wages; more than all that, for sailing-day again. Deep-voiced, long-limbed, only a little apart, he came to walk the world of the decks and ports. One of his world, he thought, he

72

turned home for St. John's. He stepped to the windy dock, that first day back, a man like other men.

Robbie. Not to be thought of under old Playfair's eyes. Yet it was here again, that raw, fresh morning. The lad came thrusting toward him across the quay, fifteen too, and tall as a man now, too. The clutter of bales and casks lay round unseen, the crowding shipmates bustled away forgotten. Robbie. The handshake came, the arm went round his shoulder, the quick, uneasy laughter troubled his ears. The eyes met, and the surge stabbed up from his depths, driving against the thumb that pressed it back. It was here now, beating in his temples now, still with that thumb of darkness pressing down. Stabbing for light, that stab of loss and longing. Always – again – for ever – let it go. Better the darkness, yes, the dark was better.

Yet it would still not go; he could not let it. The afternoon sun was warm on the rocky hill-side. They were climbing old tracks, reliving the boys' old days. All but the lost days lying dead between them. He could not stir that silence, he dared not ask; the other stirring was rising to freeze all questions. Out of those days this hunger somehow came, gagging him, growing, reaching up through his blood. Not to be named, that hunger, not to be thought of. Not to be named, not thought of. They were passing the birds'-nest places, the berry places, all the old places of the boys' remembrance, standing up clear and yet with blankness round them. They were lying on the last slope with the rock warm at their backs, the high wind singing over it, the bodies touching. That touch – that cry from the dark – his arms outstretched . . . lantern light here, the dank of the cabin round him. His face was pressed to his bunkhead, he hardly knew he had moved, till he felt the cool of the wood and the harsh breath shook him.

'Mahan – what is it, man?' Playfair braced himself on his rickety canes, startled.

What is it! The old ruin did not know what he had loosed. No sleep for Mahan, no sleep tonight again. The cold of the hill instead, the emptied place. The stinging welt of the blow, the smear of spittle. The feel of the kerchief drooping in his hand, dabbing through twilight at the mottled cheek. The thumb still

73

pressing, sealing darkness in. All of it again, those hours he had
sat alone, watching the malignant wheeling-in of night, himself
a part of night.

Playfair. Still watching. The startled exclamation hung in
the air. He tried to speak as if he had not heard it. 'I'd come back
to St. John's, paid off. And Robbie was just about to ship with
his father, done with schooling at last. So I joined him. Why
not?'

Why not? He tried to shrug, go on. But he was not yet sure
of his muscles, free of silence. Silence gripped him again. The
dock next day, the tall lads face to face, a dozen hours older, infinitely changed. Yet willing the hour that had changed them
gone, burying it fathoms deep. Risking no word; a word might
bring it back. Robbie's young voice was gruff, his young face
white. 'There'd be a berth in my father's ship,' was all he had
said, 'if ye're looking for such a thing.'

The bunk, the cool of the wood. His hands played over it
now, steadying him. He forced himself to turn, forcing a laugh.
'We'd four years together and good enough years they were,
though I'd not speak for Lije. He took me because Robbie asked
for it, but he took me down like physic. I was hard swallowing
for him, even then.

'Y'see, Playfair,' – he was lighter now, and the words were
coming easier – 'I'd a bit of a start on Robbie, and I was beginning to roughen up. You know how it is at sea. And I was coming out already in the shape I was bent to. When I found a man
in my way I got him out of it. I was a mite too quick with my
fists, and there'd be a knife in one of 'em sometimes. And I'd
learned ways to get on, or I was soon learning 'em. Ye'd find a
cargo lying about on a dock, and there was always a lad somewhere could do with a loose bale or maybe a couple of kegs. A
dark night – find the watchman a drink, hand him a clout on the
head – and there was new money in your pocket. There's many
a fine fortune been started like that, eh, Playfair? It was none of
it to Robbie's taste, but I'll say this – we'd a first run to the ice in
the old *Jeannie*, and there was talk of me and the pelts even
then –'

'Ah.'

'Ah – what?' Mahan grinned at him. 'There was nothing came of it but talk. Robbie stood up for me, cool as ever you please – lied in his father's face.'

'Not for long. You'd not have fooled old Lije on a matter of pelts. Did he send you off for that?'

'That?' The light laugh grated, and the breath was quickening again. 'I'd a year with the godly Torrances after that. And it was not pelts nor any other devilry that broke us up – it was a good deed. Could ye believe that, Playfair? How long since you've seen Malaga?'

'Malaga? It's been years. Thirty, maybe.' Playfair was gruff and curt, measuring him rather than listening.

'Then you'd not know the look of the port as it is now – nor even as it was then – it was near twelve years ago. New docks – new warehouses – all along the river there was new building – shovel-gangs, dredgers, gangs of Spanish convicts – Moors, Lascars, Chinamen, Indians, Africans, white port-scrapings that were working for a passage home – there were near two thousand of 'em there, hammering piles, scooping up mud, with steam whistles blowing, foremen cursing 'em out in a dozen tongues, horses, ox-teams, mules braying – your ears split with the racket. But that was day-time and ye didn't use the new docks then – they weren't ready. Ye lay by night tied to the old wharves, with the wine kegs piled in front of you and fruit wagons tilted over on rotten timber, and the same old heat and smells and the same old streets behind 'em. Remember those streets, Playfair? No, you'd not – not as they were then. There were ten brothels for every one in your day. There was all that scum from the works with their pay hot in their hands, and the squealing whores from half the ports of the south come to get it. And it's there that Robbie goes, looking for his first woman. Can you imagine that, Playfair? – a lad of nineteen?'

'What of it?' Playfair shrugged it away, fretful and baffled. 'It's been done enough before.'

'Ah, but not this time. No, my lad, not this time. I saw to that. I brought him back a virgin with his shirt-tail hanging out. And the harbour police so hot after us we just made the ship. It was a rescue, ye might say. But what was the thanks I got from

75

Lije Torrance? It was down to my bunk, pack my gear, and get off his ship for good. I never set foot on a deck of his again. I was off on the road for you.'

'Are ye telling me that's all?' Playfair searched incredulously through the hard, ironic vehemence. 'It's lies or nothing – ye could have saved your breath.'

'It's the truth, man – the whole truth. Robbie'd broken off by himself one night for a ramble into the town. And the old sow got her hooks onto him – well on – he was in her place when I found him. It was a different place when we left, I can tell you that.' He laughed, and the sound in the laugh made Playfair wince. 'I rumpled it up a bit, and I rumpled her. A Turk, Playfair – one o' the white Turks – with a pair of breasts like cargo slings, and a skin like mouldy cheese, and a great welt of fat circling her middle. Robbie with the likes of her – Robbie with a Turk whore! I changed the look o' those topworks, I messed that bed a bit – she'd have been carved meat the length of her if I'd not heard whistles in the street –'

'It's enough – it's enough!' Playfair lifted a cane to shut him off. He turned away, shaken and grimacing with disgust. 'I'd have done the same as Lije – I should have long ago. There's no keeping you – there's no luck in you, but –'

'But you've got me now, and you'll keep me till we get back from the ice. Is that it, old man?' Mahan grinned at him, still panting a little. 'A last good cargo of fat – ye can't let that go, can ye?'

Playfair did not answer. He knocked with a cane at the closed cabin door, and the coachman put his head in. 'We'll go now. Get me up to the deck.' His head swung round toward Mahan, slowly, painfully, for a long look. There was almost pleading in it. 'I'm – old, Mahan. Ye said it. Let be now. I'd like some peace at the end.'

'Good night, owner.' Mahan laughed softly, steady and himself once more. 'I'll fetch ye back a log-load.'

He watched the canes move out. The cabin door closed on the stone-faced Irish coachman and the hunched old pirate. The wheezing and dying pirate scared for his money now, scared for his reputation, scared of death. A man's guts crawled at the thought of him, a man wanted to vomit. His head was throbbing again.

He looked over at the bunk, and turned away. No use for that, not now. He slumped down in the chair by the cabin table, with the sextant in its case and the log-book lying beside it, its stained green cover black in the lantern light. Playfair gone now, the stir on the deck quieting. They had heaved him up to the side and lowered him over. There was the faint splash of the dory's oars in the water; the coachman rowed like a coachman.

He took the two keys from his pocket, dangled them in his hand for a minute, and unlocked the table drawer. The flat tin box came out, and he turned the other key, every motion familiar from long habit, almost without thought. There they were, the brown books, and the black books, and the red books, the stiff white letters of credit; he fanned them out in a sheaf. A man's friends, a man's anchor, a man's invincible weapon. Rothschild's Bank, London – National Shawmut, Boston – London & River Plate of Buenos Aires – Halifax Banking Company – Banco Lisboa & Acores, Lisbon – Colonial Bank of Trinidad – Colonial Bank of St. John's. Black scrolls on the white parchment of the letters, black ink in the blue, ruled columns of the books, some of it greying now. Pounds, dollars, pesos – figures in fives, tens, hundreds, even a few in thousands. Fruit of the knife, the club, the fist, the gaff, fruit of the driven ships, the luckless men. Fruit of the years since Robbie.

Robbie. Malaga. His fingers tightened on the sheaf, but the anchor would not hold. Heavy with flowers and grapes and raw new wine, hot with the harbour stink, the night came round him. He was walking down that gangway, the sea-bag over his shoulder, the blood flecks still on his jacket. The gaff swung in his hand. Somewhere a moaning trollop cursed her gashes. A shamefaced lover lurked in a cabin below, waiting his father's wrath, shaken by other thoughts. The father watched from the rail, his face in darkness. Trouble again, another shoreside brawl; the hands on the deck were grinning. Grinning and glad; this was the end of Mahan. It was the beginning of the man with the gaff.

The books, back to the books; he spread them in his hands

77

again. Strength here; all that a man could ask. A man could wash the Dogstown smell away, a man could build, a man could climb with these. A man could go where he wished, take what he wished. He had wrenched this power from the guts of the fat world. Pay for his pain here – yes – food for his hunger. Hunger. His hands went limp, the sheaf drooped in his fingers. He let the papers settle into the box, locked it, put it away. He could do nothing. He could go nowhere.

He got up, stood listening for a moment, feeling the old shell harden gratefully about him. There was silence on the deck now, and a midnight quiet was stealing over the harbour. *Kestrel* sighed, restless as old ships, even in calm, at anchor. There was not much noise from the crew; he had seen to that. The lubbers' eyes were already becoming worried; they were beginning to learn about Mahan. It was part of the spice, that teaching, and it would go on. The louts and the hard ones and the good sailors, if any; he did not know what he had and did not care. They would come back from the ice, the ones who came, broken to Mahan's way, and there would be the fun of the breaking.

Robbie. Robbie still. He struck a hand to his side; they would not go. The pounding march of the memories would not stop. The boy, the boy of the hill, the lad of the ship. The lad of the hammock slung beside his own. The breathing presence haunting the 'tween-deck nearness, the long-legged shape dim in the lantern's light. The boy gone, the gangway and the gaff. Alone with the gaff now, walking the man apart, blown on the sea-tracks, clawing through the world, clawing back always to the thought of the boy. The boy – the man – the new face hardening through the years apart, yet with that troubled warmth at every meeting. The only warmth, the only warmth there was. Once, twice, three times, perhaps, in a year the tracks would cross. The hands would meet, a tavern door would swing, rum ripple into glasses to stand undrunk, food on the plates uneaten, while the talk struggled and died. Died round the memories and the things unsaid, died round the unasked questions. Always between them still that frozen silence. Yet out of it somehow the link of pain. The boy still reached to the boy with some dim longing. There was still the bond, the one warmth in the world.

Maura. A name at first, a random, chilling breath. Suddenly a face in lamplight, her hand in Robbie's hand. The other night came round him. He had stepped ashore, hardly an hour in St. John's, with the dockside bustle slackening in summer dusk. The words came blowing from somewhere over the stir, idle, ignored, then driving down like a club — Torrance — betrothal party — Robbie Torrance to be wed. He found himself in his cabin, the sea-chest gaping open, the broadcloth coming wrinkled from its depths. Dank with disuse, he had never worn it here; the shoreside garb of the captain in the south, dickerer with merchants, doer of Playfair mischief. The face of the startled cabin boy, the smell of the iron, white linen; they blurred around him on a stony silence. He dressed without thought, fighting off thought. He found himself on the path, he was standing on the hill in darkness. He was panting and soaked with sweat, mopping the sweat from his face, carefully, lingeringly. The soaked kerchief was a weight in his hand, remindful — the other kerchief on the other hill — he put it quickly away.

The house stood up aglow from every window. Fiddle sound came to him through the open doorway. He neared it, crossed the threshold. The warmth of the home he had never seen was round him. He stood amid it infinitely apart, ultimately adrift, the last anchor cut. Lije Torrance came to him. Robbie came to him. He came with Robbie to the side of the girl. Her voice spoke to him and her eyes withdrew from him, infinitely withdrawing too, her hand in that hand. The dancers stamped and glowed, her face glowed, raised to that face. He held his glass and watched. The summer night was black beyond the doorway. The scraping fiddles reeled and shrieked about him. He felt the last cold creeping down to his heart.

The face. The fiddle shriek. He stumbled from them down the hill to the dock. He lived a week out hearing the fiddles still, over the groan of winches, the thud of bales. Another week; the slings came lurching down, the casks rocked through the hatches, the last hatch closed. Old cargo off, new on; he could lift away. Make work, mend rigging, paint; he could not go yet. Robbie. The girl. A week to the wedding now. The ship lay at the dock, the Playfairs fumed. The hands stood idle, the lines hung over the bollards, the master walked in the port. Day-time,

79

night-time, from the cheerful streets of the merchants to the high lanes of the hill, he passed with the gaff in hand, restless as wind. To his deck again, and the silent cabin again, and another silent leaving, while the crew gaped behind him. Three days now – Robbie gone to the girl. Robbie gone to the girl, wedding or not. Robbie gone. Malaga – the hot, soft, sour-sweet stench of a brothel haunted the wind. The gashed whore – a woman too – he had had his pay of her. Maura – no mending here, but pay at least for his pain, loss for his loss. Another day gone, night come. Night and the Bartlett gate; he was passing that gate again. He saw the face in the window, the white of the throat, the loose robe, the rippling play of the comb in the yellow hair. He marked the fence and the tree.

Next day the master did not stir from the ship; there was no need. From his cabin on the last night he heard the step on deck. He did not move. Nothing to change now. A dozen hours and pain would swallow pain, the scream would tear at silence. After that? His thoughts stopped there. The boots chunked on the ladder, the shoulders loomed in the doorway. Tomorrow's bridegroom. He got to his feet, the smile steady on his lips, the hand out. 'Well, Robbie! – you're a lad aglow with joy.'

He lied and knew it, yet the joy was there, fire under ashes, struggling to be free. The old struggle; the face in the shadowy lantern light was heavy with the old look.

'I've not been aboard before,' Torrance was saying, 'though you'll guess I've thought about it. I knew you were in, but –' The words halted and strayed, groping for something else they could not reach. 'I know it's not been all smooth with us in the past, but I'd like ye to be there at the church. She'd like it – I've just come from her.'

Warm from her touch still, warm from her lips. The smile stayed warm and wide on the other lips, the lilt grew in the voice. 'Your lass, Robbie? She'll have me there? Now that's a rare one – and a Bartlett too. Are ye *sure* ye speak for her?'

The truth was plain enough in Torrance's eyes, but he struggled on. 'I'd like all shipshape, all well with the world – I suppose it's how a man feels at a time like this. I'd like it to be – well – a sort of mending between us, Tim – I've no way else to say it. I've too much, it seems; I've always had – now above all. If there was anything I could do for ye – share with ye –'

The shrug ended it, helpless and groping still. The bottle came to the table, the glasses clinked in the toast. They walked to the gangway together, parted with a nod and a laugh, while the shriek of another laughter beat at silence. Share! Aye, sharing there would be at last. The scream would tear the silence, tearing all. And after that? His thoughts still stopped. Plunging and wheeling, wild as storm-blown gulls, they hovered at that brink.

She had not screamed. Crushed to the bloody bed, the joy torn out of her she had lain, payment for all. Not all, not yet. Beyond her now the years of the emptied world, not to be borne, not to be borne alone. Robbie – let Robbie come. He had waited for the cry from her, the rush of the boots outside, the door smashed open, Robbie's hand at his throat. He had felt his own hands closing around that throat, seen the wild eyes as naked as his own. Naked and stripped – naked and stripped together they would go. No cry. No sound at the door. The breeze at the window softly stirring lace. The white, stained body – still.

There had been silence only. There had been the white, set face in the church. There had been the seven years. Bound to the one end now, he knew it well. He had seen it, wanted it, and hovered back, toying with ships and filling books with figures, toying with Robert Torrance. Let it come now, let it come now, he had thought a dozen times. Strike and be done, strike and be done and gone, the anguish told him. Still he had waited.

Let it come now, he had thought that night last year. He had dropped to the ice to bring it. Tall in the moonless quiet, idling at familiar mischief, he had heard the other step. He had straightened, knife in hand. Robbie. The waiting ended. Yet – Robbie gone? Suddenly he had known he could not face it yet.

Not Robbie. It had been the old man. Sick of the long years too, and come to end them. The old man clinging still around the son, suddenly unbearable as the thought of the wife. The deep eyes searching and the old voice hard, knowing too much, too much to be borne by Mahan. He had struck cleanly, surely, and with carelessness and relief. He had walked back, lighter, to the silent ship, savouring the respite, knowing it was the last. Robbie's turn now; Robbie, and all would end. Bury the hunger with the bones and rot; empty the world and walk alone in it, the man with the gaff, freed. He let himself settle slowly onto the bunk, stretched out, his eyes widening on darkness. Soon now – the man with the gaff, freed. Yet now – even now – to walk that dark alone –?

TORRANCE drew up, a stone chunking away from him under the last thrust of his boot. He listened idly to the click on the sloping rock face, the stir of following pebbles, and then the faint splash. Perhaps he imagined the splash; he did not know. He seemed to have lost all sureness.

There was the chill on the cliff now of the moments when false dawn gives way for a while to deeper darkness. The tide boomed in the throat of the cove, a hundred feet beneath him. The gleam of the ice-blink in the north, heralding the floe, seemed filled with pale menace. He was bone-cold, weary as death, and every familiar sound came to him with a dim mutter of warning.

The ice-blink began to fade as the glimmer of real dawn grew along the horizon. He sniffed the wind instinctively, and instinctively his heart lifted at the thought of the pet day coming. The smell of the floe came down to him in the light breeze, and as the sun strode inward a white glitter twinkled beyond the blue of the inshore water. The strung-out pans of slob ice were nearer than they had been yesterday. They were already gliding by, the floe's outriders. Behind them, above Baccalieu and Bonavista and the Funks and the Horse Islands, along all the miles of the Newfoundland coast, and around the shoulder of the Labrador, the ice was moving down from the darkness of the Pole. Cradled in the arms of the great current it came, a continent that was neither sea nor land, bound for the southward sun and dissolution. The northbound ships lay in the harbour below, hidden from him here by the high shoulder of the hill. Nearly four thousand men of the city and the outports, the Tickles and the Guts and the Reaches and the Coves of Newfoundland, were bound to the age-old rendezvous of the ships and the moving ice. They were snoring under the decks of their vessels now, or climbing aboard them, blear-eyed and quarrelsome from the last night ashore. He was a Torrance, and no living man of Newfoundland could remember a sealing season when there had not been a Torrance in command, or standing in the mainmast barrel of one of the ships. Men of good memory, all of them; trusted with other men's lives, and keeping faith.

A thread of wood-smoke climbed from the chimney of the house. It would soon be time to go. There would be fish boiling in the iron pot and tea on the stove now, and bread and butter and molasses set out on the clean oilcloth of the table. Maura would be gathering the bits and oddments to go in the sea-bag, readying the last of his gear. She would look at him with her eyes heavy from staring into the dark, as he was gaunt and haggard from his night on the cliff. But it would change nothing; nothing could be changed now.

He started for the house, heavily. Below the first rocky ledge the frames of the flakes stood beside the crazy lean-to of the gutting-shed and the smell of salt and fish was brisk on the air. On the slope beyond the house the snow had not yet left the thin and starving soil that clung on the rocks and yielded up so grudgingly its few turnips and potatoes. So grudgingly, for so much work, yet the work went on. It seemed he could still feel the blisters raised by the hoe-handle on his soft, ten-year-old hands. The hands of Elijah Torrance had felt them too, the ten-year-old before him. For a moment as he looked he hated it all, each bare, remembered foot of it. It spoke too stingingly, this world of the boy's first memories, of all that was gone with the boy.

He came into the house and there was the clean oilcloth and the heavy, shining white of the dishes, the white bread and the yellow butter and the pans hung on the wall above the stove gleaming in the morning sunlight. And Maura and her slim body, and the love that ached in each and joined them still. And silence. Only her step, the little clack of plates, the even ticking of the tall old clock in the parlour, broke the silence.

He took off his cap and jacket, flung them over a chair, and

86

sat at the table. He had not eaten since the noon before and for a while he filled himself like a wolf, famished and sullen. When he was finished he sat back in his chair. He sipped his tea and looked straight ahead of him through the doorway into the little parlour shining like a ship's cabin. A great walrus-tusk surrounded by tiny figures carved from whales' teeth by Eskimos at the top of the Labrador stood on the table inlaid with a thousand pieces of sandalwood that his great-great-grandfather had brought from India. Maura moved beside the stove, then sat at the table facing him, pretending to sip her tea.

It was good, it was all so good. The warm, tight house and the shining cleanliness of it, the old strong sureness of the lives lived here before them. They were inheritors of it all, a part of it all, cherishing it, continuing it. He looked at her in the sunny morning light and a slow rage rose in him. They had talked nightmares, lived nightmares. This was his own, the son of Elijah Torrance. He had robbed no one to gain it, he wronged no one in loving it. All that he looked at here, this was his life. A man would keep it. A man would stay with it, possess it, and there was no staying.

He could not say all or any of it. The words died against her silence and the nightmares came again, nightmare on nightmare, breeding from the night's sickness. She would hear nothing, understand nothing, and in the end Tim Mahan would have her. He would have all this if he wanted it, to sell, or wreck, or destroy. Looking at her averted face the new and monstrous thought took shape for the first time. He felt the cold helplessness of a jammed ship, moving like the ice itself in the flow of the great current. They had been borne so far already, monstrously far. There was no holding ground and still the current ran, sinuous and deadly. She did not know that man. If he came back from the ice Robert Torrance would not, and if he came ... Torrance would not think of it. He got up.

She rose to her feet with him. For a while, as he collected gaff and knives and climbed into sealskin boots, she moved about the kitchen and to and from the bedroom and the shed, putting the heavy sweaters and the socks and the rest into his duffle bag. They spoke quietly of little things with the great thing silent

87

between them. Once she paused with something in her hands and her head bent over it. He waited, but she could not steel herself to speak. Her hand went to his shoulder and slid down the length of his sleeve, but her eyes still looked away from him. She moved away herself.

Even as he stood in the doorway with his bag shouldered, even as he kissed her and she clung to him with her whole body calling on him to stay and live, she could not find the words. He put her from him at last, gently, and she looked up. 'I shall be watching from the cliff.'

'I know.' He looked over her head for a moment into the shining peace of the home. Then he turned, as a restless braying of sirens rose from the harbour. She was standing behind him in the open doorway, there was rock and sunlight ahead, and he was striking down for the city.

He came out from the foot of the path onto the flag-hung bustle of Water Street and pushed along with the crowd. The backslappers slapped him, and the shouters shouted his name, and he answered them all absently, shrugging their hands off. Men, women, and children out of school, the rich and poor, the great and small were streaming down for the docks. There were splayed boots and carriage wheels sucking together in the slush, and bunting whipped above them from the stores lining the street. The doors of the merchants and chandlers were all locked; there would be no business today. The big houses on the hill stood up in the chilly sunlight, windows gaping, doors flung open, with maids and mistresses all waving together. The quays were a rowdy carnival of shouts and shoving and laughter, and Torrance was swept along with the wave of the latecomers hurrying to join their ships. He caught a glimpse of Bracebridge bellowing something from his carriage, but there was no time for him now and he could not hear anyway. There was no need to hear; he could see that the old man's worries were washed away by excitement. His own were leaving him too as he neared his berth. Beyond the Bracebridge quay the ships swung in the harbour, each with a last hook down, iron-nosed, sooty with coal dust, bellowing and gay like the town. He stood for a moment eyeing the pack from habit, savouring it all from habit, and then he was alongside *Jean Bright*.

She loomed up, deep-waisted, twin-masted, with the tall funnel amidships, cluttered and noisy as all the other vessels, and homely and familiar. She still had her gangway down, and as he came onto the seething deck the men made way for him with an easy, bustling respect. There were many of the old hands there, his father's men. He caught the eyes of a few and found nothing in them but perhaps a touch of sympathy. In spite of last year, and in spite of yesterday's folly, they were glad to be sailing with a Torrance.

He went below to his cabin, tossed his bag on the bunk, and clattered up topside again. It was good to feel that chunk of cleats on the iron ladder, to fill his nostrils with the stink of old fat and new coal. The sea mood was taking over. All about him now lines were being cast off or anchors hauled inboard. Steam-and-sailers all, the ships lay low in the water, bunkered to the eyes with coal, and ballasted with the rocks that would go overboard as the seal pelts came aboard. Foot-square baulks of timber and mountains of stores and gear littered all the decks, for there was no stowage below. The men would sleep in the holds with their skins or blankets spread on the bare, wet planks. Later, if the luck came, they would sleep on the slime and blubber of frozen fat. All through the rigging and along the lower yards hung sides of bacon waiting the cook's knife. They hung in every ship, and streaming out above them, bowsprit to peak to stern, meaningless and gleeful as the uproar round them, flapped all the signal pennants the lockers boasted.

There was little for Torrance to do. Ernest Johns, grinning with excitement himself, came up to report all shipshape, and when Johns said that, it was so. The two of them watched from the wheel-house as the gangway came in and the last line looped from the jetty and was coiled. 'Slow astern.' Torrance gave his first order, the answer came up the voice-pipe, and there was the soft shudder of the engines. They were easing off now, bows were swinging in the harbour and smoke belching from the funnels. A kind of silence ran along the quays, and then from behind the crowd, high in its old brick casemate, the town clock struck ten. From the hill came a grey puff and the boom of an ancient gun, and then it was all the sirens and bells and throats of the port together.

The smoke from the ships billowed up and the wakes began to cross in a turmoil of seething water. It looked good to the town, if it meant nothing else, to be the first vessel out. Old skippers, with their thoughts on shares and log-loads, were content to take their time. But there were always a few young bachelors standing at some of the voice-pipes with their girls watching them from shore. They set the pace and the rest were forced to keep up with it from sheer pride or sheer self-preservation. The battle was on as usual. In a shouting, jeering confusion of climbing bow waves, scraping sides, and splintering spar tips, the tangle of vessels was sorting itself out, becoming a stringy pack. Torrance found himself grinning, yelling, and cursing with the other captains as he wove in and out, ducking the charging bows, edging away for the Narrows. The first ship raced through the gap well ahead of him, then another and another. He was eighth or ninth in the line as he made the harbour mouth and the smoke began to lift. *Kestrel* was still astern with the rest of the pack; he did not know how far and he did not care. He was clear of the Pancake, clear of the Chain Rock. The wind from the outside struck, the scend of the sea came, and he was swinging hard to port.

Hard to the north. It moved in his blood for a moment, this annual migration of men outward and northward to meet the southern-moving ice and the seals. It caught him out of himself, lifted him to the cold fellowship of the winds and tides, the sea-beasts and the living food they followed. It went on, it went on for ever, and he lived and breathed, a part of it.

Deep in the sea and writhing out from the Pole, the mighty Labrador Current set toward the south, the winds and storms scarring the surface above it, contending always vainly with the relentless southern flow. And riding gripped in its arms came the great, thousand-mile-square ice raft fed from the polar seas and northern glaciers. It was moving toward him now, treacherous, deadly, unpredictable, making its own weather, driven aside by cross-winds of its own breeding, yet always returning to the southward route. Its vast expanses cracked apart and rejoined. Its ageless bergs, snapped off from the seaward-crawling fingers of the Greenland Cap, towered amid jagged dunes, contemptuously smashing out great lakes for themselves as they moved with sinister docility to the wind and sea. Frozen rain and snow, even now, would be adding glittering miles to the floe's breadth as it moved down from Baffin Bay and beyond Cape Mercy toward the Labrador coast. Islands of fresh-water ice from the mouths of emptying rivers would be joining as the sun warmed. Formations of pulpy sludge-ice would be crawling out ahead to warn of the coming and some were already here. The first finger-ends and fringes he had seen from the cliff this morning lay off to starboard now.

He watched them thicken about him, always on the move. Beyond them, days to the north, the solid white desert groaned southward in majestic agony, breaking and rejoining in a thoussand jigsaw patterns. And somewhere within that huge and desolate expanse the seals came, riding the great raft as they had always done, whelping on the ice at a season that had varied by hardly so much as a week in all the years that any man had known. They came as the ice came, they moved as the seas moved; and the men went out to meet them, locked in the same iron rhythm.

Yet, always within the pattern, was the luck and skill of the game. Torrance had learned the way of it for twenty years, watching the winters with his father. He had watched alone last winter. The seals whelped where the ice pleased them as their time came, looking always for the glitter of frozen rain and the white of fresh snow. Their young whimpered and died on the wind-swept bareness of steely polar ice; they were eaters and drinkers of snow, and snow was their nesting-place. Where the snow came, and when, and how it lay, where of a thousand patches the seals might have chosen one, was the winter guess of the sealer. Far-off weather and wind, infinitely varied, changing in intricate sequence from year to year, governed the hunting and finding. One sat in the south and watched, and guessed of the north.

There had been 'Green Bay' springs when some mysterious relenting sent the ice down early and the seals came far to the south. In those years, as the floe drove in on the coast and the ships rode north outside it, they often rode short-handed, with

91

some men left behind them and others leaving as they went. Standing beside his father on *Jean Bright*'s deck, Torrance had watched the home-stayers starting out from the shore, off on their own across the bobbing cakes of ice, leaping from raft to raft, testing the treacherous clefts and watery sish in front of them with their long-handled gaffs, as carelessly sure-footed as goats on a hill-side. He had heard Lije Torrance curse and then chuckle helplessly as pans brushed the side and his men piled over onto them, streaming away like schoolboys at the first touch of a footing or the sight of a bobbing-hole. Sometimes, later, he had helped to pick them up, marooned on tossing islands that were cracking apart beneath them, or huddled like stormbound sheep in a driving blizzard. There would be none of that this year; this was no Green Bay spring. It had been a winter like the year before, troublingly like, with the same steady march of relentless cold. Once more, as last year, only the first faint tracings of the floe were southward yet. The ice lay well off the coast and the Inside Cut was open, a broad lane of water reaching up for the craggy head of the island and the coast of the Labrador.

Ahead and astern now the pack was strung out under a thinning haze of smoke. The last ship had cleared the Narrows and the sirens and cheers had died away. The sun was bright on blue water and a blaze on the ice to starboard, but there was a dun air of business settling over the vessels. One by one the gaudy clusters of pennants dropped from the halyards. Sails, black with coal smoke, bellied out from yards and cross-trees to help while the wind held. Each captain was on his own now, driving up the Cut with all the speed he could make and already watchful of the others. There would be a day or two yet to think, worry, and remember the winter's signs, to guess at the ways of this year's ice and seals. Then there would be the day when the ice thickened to starboard and the bows began to swing. The lazy men and the optimists would go first as always and come home early and empty. Others would not sheer off for a week or more, but sooner or later they would all be twisting among the lanes of the floe or smashing their way forward by main strength of bow and engines. And somewhere ahead for the lucky ones, the seals waited. Somewhere in that white mystery that was still only a glint in the northward sunlight, the sleek brown beast with the tearful, speaking eyes and the curious harp-shaped markings on their backs slithered and barked at the bobbing-holes with their new-born young beside them.

He had left Johns with the helmsman as soon as they cleared the harbour. Now, standing on the after deck in the warm and breezy sunlight, he smelt the sea and the ice and found it good. It was good to see sail above the funnel smoke for a bit; it would be down soon enough when the ships could not run free. The sing of his own taut canvas overhead was oddly soothing, linking him dimly and pleasantly with the other days of grandfathers and great-grandfathers. The sleepless night was behind him and had left its mark. He felt a strange, numb lightness; he seemed unmoored from himself. The sun and sea flowed into him, he rose and fell with the ship, a part of the great cycle, ageless and infinite. A man's life and death in all this were less than a falling snowflake; pain and loss flowed by, shadows of shadows. Elijah Torrance – Tim Mahan – Robert Torrance – they came and went together, nothing together, lost in the blind greatness. Maura – her face rose before him, standing as he had left her at the door, and yet his thought would not fasten on her. She seemed to float in his mind, dreamily apart, flowing away like the wake. Maura –

'*Kestrel*, sor! – are ye leaving that damned Jinker to get the foot of us?' It was Hardy pushing at his elbow, one of the best of the old hands, with a dozen men around him and more coming. The deck seemed to be emptying itself aft and the port rail was lined three deep as far forward as he could see. He had been conscious of the rising murmur, he had seen and not seen the thrust of sail astern and the big, blunt bow pushing out from among his followers. Now the vessel was nearer, barely a cable's length off, with the wash climbing along the black hull. She was going to pass, and pass so close aboard she would cut the *Jean Bright*'s wind.

He straightened, measuring the distance, his eye on the closing gap. 'What's the matter with you all?' he said coolly. 'There's time enough and room enough – we're not in the ice yet. Let her go if she wants to.'

He saw Johns by the helmsman and he saw him give the order. The ship wore over a point as the other came ploughing up, and for a moment the gap widened. Then it began to close as *Kestrel*'s heaving bow came inching along by the quarter and her side heeled inward, so recklessly, so deliberately, that the tip of her foremast yard-arm locked with the yard-tip of *Jean Bright*. The sound of splintering wood came from above, there was a furious shout from the men, and then a great blast from *Kestrel*'s siren as she wrenched free and passed. For a moment, as they ate her funnel smoke, he had a quick glimpse of the wheel-house and of Mahan himself at the wheel, grinning and waving. Then it was over. *Kestrel* was clear and standing on ahead, with all the oaths of Newfoundland trailing after her.

Torrance pushed out from the angry huddle of men with his face carefully blank. He climbed to the quarter-deck and watched as Johns squared the ship away and sent up a splicing party to mend the damage. When they were running free again the old man joined him. There was gloom enough mixed with the anger in his face, but there was also a hint of relief. *Kestrel*'s patched, grey-white sails were standing lower on the horizon, and the acrid taste of her smoke was blown away. 'Well ahead now and pleased with himself,' said Johns grimly. 'But it's good riddance if we've seen the last of him.'

'We've not, but let him go.' Torrance felt a lifting, almost gay defiance. Snowflake and spume-fleck, locked in the iron rhythm, each was bound to his end. One would go down and both at last go down before the power that moved the seas and the great ice.

HE was growing hazy and sleepy as Cape St. Francis fell away astern, wanting his bunk and not wanting it. The air was good and the sense of freedom persisted. He was not yet gripped by the hard demands of routine. In the warmth of the late noon sun, his very tiredness was a kind of grateful relief. The ship seemed to sail herself under the touch of a few old hands while the rest of the crew idled, waiting the sorting out. That would be Ernest Johns's work, and he was always leisurely about it in the first hours of a voyage, giving the excitement time to die away. The worst of the ruck on deck had been cleared off, and most of the idling men were drifting below. There was still a great clutter of gear and stores, and the stacks of timber lay waiting to be hammered up into pounds, but there was no hurry about that. The bins would go up only when pelts were sighted. Along the port bulwarks a few of the outport men were still watching the shoreline and the last lonely little clusters of roofs and docks. But their home coves were behind them and the coast was emptier now.

From the holds Torrance could hear the usual arguments about gear and bunk space, and the growlings of hungry men wanting their dinner. He listened idly and knowledgeably with an eye on the cook's galley. The door opened and Eben Gravely came out of it, seventy years old, bristling already with a week's grey stubble, and biting on a rancid pipe. Balanced on his shoulder was a great tin platter of his Figgy Duffs, balls like doughy roundshot, baked the night before and stuffed with raisins. He walked the length of the deck, came to the forward hatch, and dumped his load without ceremony onto the heads and shoulders below. That was dinner, so far as he was concerned. The cans for tea would be filled when he was squared away in the galley. Torrance grinned as the hungry bellowings wafted the old man back, quite unmoved. Sailing-day as usual. He took a last look about him and made for the companionway.

Ernest Johns, in the cabin next to his own, was bent over rosters and watch-bills. The eternal black pipe drooped from his mouth. 'Well boy,' he looked up and smiled. 'Off agin. It feels good.'

'It does at that.' Torrance came in and glanced over his shoulder at the laboriously written signatures and the X-marks of the crew-list. 'They're a likely enough lot, I'd say by the look of 'em.'

'Aye. Good for a long, hard run.'

'They'll get it. Seals'll be high this year.'

Johns went on with his work, soberly non-committal. It was not for him to say where the seals might be. The captain's guess was his own, the most jealously guarded of his rights and the sharpest test of a man. Sealers looked to a good captain with a kind of fanatic trust. 'I was thinking,' he said at last, shoving the papers away from him, carefully casual, 'might be a good idea to take our time for a bit. Save coal.'

Torrance looked at him quizzically. 'You're not thinking of coal. Say what's in your mind.'

'Well, if the run's as long as last year it'll take us near to our limit. That's one thing.'

'Aye. And what else?'

The old man lit his pipe deliberately and expelled a long, acrid puff. 'He's ahead now. Leave him get well ahead. Many a laggard ship's been first to the patch.'

'I've not seen it in my time. And we'll not see it this year.' Torrance felt his knees buckling, the tiredness in him gathering like a cold weight; the good mood was gone. 'We're out for fat. And we'll go for it at our own speed.'

Johns shrugged and his face went blank again. He got up with his sheaf of papers. 'Into your cabin, boy – you could do with some sleep. I'll rout out the hands.'

As he dropped down on his bunk Torrance heard the first bark for the marshalling of the watches, and then the yelling and

98

stamping as the men poured up from the holds. Cheerful men, as cheerful as any in the fleet. The *Jean Bright*, for them, was still a lucky ship, and the men who sailed with a Torrance were still envied. It was a good thought and a bad one, and his eyes closed with it. When he came topside again it was to the starry chill of a March night.

For three days the ships ran up the Cut in fine weather. On the fourth day the thinning out began. Three ships turned for the ice in the late morning, two in the afternoon. Just at sunset *Kestrel* stood up ahead, wallowing under her funnel smoke and edging away to starboard. Trouble, the men said hopefully as the *Jean Bright* neared her, or else she was turning off for the ice too; she was not using her speed. Then darkness fell like a blanket, thickened by the first touch of fog, and in the morning she was nowhere to be seen. They were meeting heavier ice in the Cut itself now, and all the canvas came in. It would be steam only from now on. Yesterday the pans and clumps of sludge had drifted by like rafts in the sea; today the sea flowed in lakes and rivulets among a moving land of ice. Late in the afternoon Torrance gave the order for starboard helm. There were ships ahead of him, still bound up the Cut, and ships astern that gave no sign of swinging, but this was his choice. It was time to enter the floe.

He left the deck and climbed to the barrel swaying at the foremast head. Already Hardy, master of the first hunting-watch, had been posted to the mizzen-barrel, and his eyes were combing the floe. Fifty feet below, the crew milled along the bulwarks and Ernest Johns was standing beside the helmsman, calmly puffing his pipe. Torrance waved to him, then braced himself for the first shattering jar of pan ice against the ship's side.

It came, and around him the horizon rose and fell as his barrel wheeled with the mast-peak. Ahead in the sunlight the floe was a dazzling mass of white, wrinkled and cratered with blue water, rising here and there to the hump of a raft or the pinnacle of a berg. For a while he scunned the ship himself, shouting down to the helmsman the orders that brought the iron-and-timbered bow around the larger cakes or sent it surging over the smaller ones. In an hour his head ached with the lurching and jarring, he was bruised in a dozen places and grimly exultant from the work. Whatever the trip might bring, this was his trade, his life. He was living it.

They came into a long patch of open water and he was no longer needed above. He put his telescope to his eye and swept the horizon. Three or four blots of smoke lifted to the north in the Cut, from ships still carrying on. There were two or three to the south-east of him, already deep in the ice. And there was another smudge, almost directly astern, hovering along the twists of the lane he had made. He watched for a moment as the rise of masts and the lines of the hull came clear. Then he put away the telescope, called for a man from below, and swung himself to the deck. Wherever *Kestrel* had been through the foggy night she was hard on his tail now, entering the floe in his wake.

Hardy was bellowing angrily from the mizzen-barrel, announcing the fact to the crew. The men eyed Torrance sullenly as he dropped down among them, but he made his face say nothing. All afternoon they had an easy passage through light ice. By evening they were well in and set for the north again. The heavy work would be likely to start in the morning. He had no hope, like the southward ships, of an early meeting with seals, and the ships still north in the Cut were not going to find an easier entrance. It was going to be the same as last year, or harder. Toward dark as he stood by the bulwark sipping a mug of tea, he saw Johns at the after rail with a telescope to his eye, surrounded by a group of the men, muttering and pointing. He called him forward, irritably. 'Will you let be with that glass! You know who it is, and the more you make of it the more you upset the lads.'

'Aye. You've the right of it.' Johns was gloomily repentant. 'But I can't shut the men away from the after deck, and they don't like what they see.'

The ship moved through the night, nibbling its way carefully. By morning, as they bit deeper into the floe, the ice came heavier and darker. The bruising, crushing, forward struggle went on as the watches changed in the barrels. The course held north by east, but hour after hour the ship zigzagged along the open cracks in the floe, riding down the drifting pans, rocking as they bucked beneath her. The decks shivered with the thrust of the engines, the scream of the safety-valves cut shrilly above the suck and rush of water. Ice, moving with the light breeze, locked close against the sides and churned away before the blunt thrust of iron. *Jean Bright* lifted and grated over the pans, swayed and climbed and settled as they broke beneath her and the crackling fragments swirled out muddily astern. The sun disappeared late in the afternoon and the steely daylight closed in about them. The limitless expanse ahead took on a sinister greyness, and still trailing them astern was the ragged column of smoke. The off-watch men were drifting aft once more, gathering in fretful knots, watching it.

'Bastard!' Johns had been standing quietly beside Torrance, but the word broke from him abruptly. 'We'd not a sight of him last year till he came onto us in the patch. This time it's worse.'

'Did ye expect anything else? I should have stuck to my first notion. I should have stayed home this year.'

'No.'

'No, is it? And it was no from Maura too. Have ye been having a word with her?'

'I have not. Not since the day we set the stone in the graveyard.' Johns did not turn his head. He had watched the courtship, watched the faces at the wedding, watched afterward. One dared not imagine all he knew or guessed. But he had shut it away from him now. 'She's right, boy, if she said it. You're here in the ice because it's the way of your life. There's no changing it.'

Torrance swept a hand fretfully over the scarred wood of the bulwark. 'Sometimes I feel I'm battling all the lot of you. You talk all ways at once. Come to the ice but have no trouble with him – leave all be as it is! D'ye think *he* will?'

'I think it'll be your choice.' The old man raised his eyes to him, steady and hard. 'And you're captain here with a ship and a crew to think of. You're not your own man.'

The night came down and they nosed ahead cautiously in the thick darkness, fearing a change of weather. But the dawn broke with patches of blue sky shredding the grey cloudbanks,

101

and they were battering forward again. For two more days and two nights under the half-disc of a waxing moon, the shouts of the scunner in the barrel were repeated by the helmsman below and the ship jolted and swerved in response to them. By the eighth morning the shallow glitter of southern ice was giving way to the dun grey of the north; it was polar ice about them, diamond-hard and deadly. The mood of the men was sharpening. There was more cursing over Gravely's pork and duffs. There were more arguments at each watch-change and too many fist-fights blazing up in the hold. With the dark ice came the seal-hunger and the usual fears and impatience, but beyond that there was the trail of smoke astern. Some of the old hands were muttering about the voyage last year, and the new men were listening. Johns came to the cabin with the word of it on the ninth night.

'Lads are getting a bit restless, Robbie.'

Torrance was stretched on his bunk, rocking from side to side with the plunging ship. He nodded. 'Thinking they've come with the wrong man, are they? Well, they might have the truth of it there.'

'I've heard nothing of that – not from one of 'em.'

'But it's in their minds, and you know it. The off-watch lads live on the after deck, watching that funnel smoke. And then they look at me. What do they expect me to do? Swing round and sink him?'

'I said they were restless. I didn't say they were daft.' Johns knocked out his pipe and shoved it into his pocket, irritably. 'And I'd only one thought.'

'Well?'

'There'll be a dark night soon. The weather can't hold like this. And a wind, maybe. If it came right and set the ice to shifting there might be a good clear stretch of water opened up. We could maybe give him the slip.'

Torrance glowered at him with morose scorn. 'All the ifs in the world to it, and no good anyway. We'd lose him for a day, perhaps, maybe two, and he'd be hard onto us again.'

Johns fumbled vaguely for his pipe, took it out and looked at it, and stuffed it back once more. 'How many days d'ye think we have left to go?'

'To seal-sign? I'd say a full week, maybe a day less. Near to our limit, anyway – same as last year.'

It was a measure of Johns's concern that he had asked the question at all. His face grew grave at the answer. Torrance sat up and swung his feet to the deck. 'Well, what is it? What's in your mind now? Is it my fault that Mahan hangs on in my wake?'

'No. And I'm not speaking of faults.' The old man eyed him steadily. 'I say we've a chance to lose him.'

'And I say not.'

'All right. But you're showing more of the strain than you think you are. Can you hold onto yourself?'

'I've come for the fat and I'll get it,' Torrance said gruffly. 'Go back to the swabs out there and tell 'em so.'

'I'll do that.' Johns turned for the door, gruff himself. 'There's nothing wrong with the men that the fat won't cure.'

The fat. The men. Torrance lay back on the bunk. The old man's words had brought up the smoke again, fogging his thoughts with it. He stirred restlessly, angrily, struggling to break free. Somewhere ahead were the Harps, with the furry balls of the Whitecoats whimpering beside them. Thousands and thousands of them together, they lay spread out in the pack, and the circle reached from its centre to the limit of every horizon. Yet for all its ragged vastness it would be a speck in the greater vastness of the moving floe. A dozen ships would miss it. Others would come too late. Only the lucky few would go home with the log-loads that meant firewood and food and gear for the summer's fishing, or a new roof on the house, or planks for a tumbling dock. Flour and pork in the larder, a few shillings to the chandler, debts going down not up; that was prosperity to the men of the landwash shacks and the little outport houses. It hung on the captain's guess, on his seal-sense, and his nerve, and sometimes their lives hung with it. If it hung now on a mind haunted and blurred, dimmed by that following smoke ...

He fell asleep with the thought, and woke with it. He stood with it through the cold hours of the middle watch, eyeing the blot astern as it swayed after him under a half moon. But he put it from him in the morning and held it grimly away. The ship groaned and butted on; the day passed. Except for the cloud in his wake there was no smoke on any horizon. He had lost the other vessels. Some would be a hundred miles to the north now, some as far south, but that thought did not shake him. He was sure of himself once more; he could find the fat.

He came up from breakfast in the morning to find a following wind blowing acrid wisps from *Kestrel* over his own deck. She had closed up to barely a mile, but there was not much time to watch her. The ice had been hardening steadily through the night. About mid morning *Jean Bright* came to a sudden, jarring stop. Bergs rode along the horizon and all around the ship were the steely-grey humps of polar packs. She had been nosing carefully down a narrow channel of the floe and had just come in sight of a wider lake opening beyond when the wind shifted. Smoothly and swiftly, like the sliding bar of a trap, the ice closed in ahead and then astern. The lane of water fore and aft of the ship had become a bucking ridge of ice.

'Jammed!' The shout ran along the deck, and there was a scuffle below as the off-watch men turned out. Johns was leaning far out over the forward bulwark, studying the restless blocks grinding together and piling up ahead. He glanced aft, measured the position there, and turned with a volley of orders. The men of the first watch scrambled over the bulwarks and slithered about on the ice, grabbing up tools that came tumbling down after them. Axes and crow-bars, picks and chisels were being heaved over by the second watch, lined along the rails. Then the dynamiters began to drop over the side, chewing their lighted pipes, tossing their boxes along as if they were bricks. No use to go bellowing after them, Torrance knew, preaching the virtues of caution. The lighted pipe and the powder went together for the old hands, a kind of a badge of nerve. 'Never been blown up yit, sor,' was the best answer he would get; 'and sarved under better masters,' as a sulky additional comment when he turned his back.

Twenty men of the third watch were already paying out a long hawser from the bow and spacing themselves on the ice along its length. The eighty-odd men still on board pushed back in a three-deep mass along the starboard bulwark. Johns eyed

104

his arrangements, cursed a laggard or two, and then bellowed an order. The men strung along the hawser began to heave. The men on deck charged from the starboard to the port side and came up with a thundering stamp. The ship shuddered with it and bucked forward a few feet to the pull of the hawser. Ice sucked and gurgled along the water line, then closed in again.

'Loosened her a bit,' Johns said calmly. Torrance stood beside him, saying nothing. The master's authority gave way here to the old man's seventy years and his certain knowledge of the ice. And Johns was not much worried.

'In with the line.' He was barking crisply to the men on the bow hawser. 'Make her fast astarn and pay her out. Ahoy there, you with the powder –' his voice lifted easily over the commotion to reach the dynamite gang laying their long fuses, 'are ye ready?'

'Down and set, Ernest!'

'Light her up!'

A match scraped and flared, a swift twinkle raced along the ice, and men came running from it to scramble aboard the ship. 'Full astarn! Heave astarn there!' Johns's shout soared up again. The ship was rocking astern to the push of the engines and the pull of the hawser as the last of the breathless dynamiters tumbled over the side. The explosive went up ahead in a gurgling, lofting bubble of flying chunks. The hawsermen let go, and the engines reversed in a cloud of smoke and steam. The loosened ship, with a new forward burst, ground its nose into the narrow, weltering crack opened by the dynamite. Almost at the same moment the wind veered again, the clutching edges of the crack gave way, and the ice with malevolent playfulness opened out in a long, easy channel.

For a moment the panting men laughed and swore over the waste of work and powder. They swore again, with none of the laughter in it, as they looked back to see *Kestrel* riding up easily behind them through a clear, open lane. Then everything else was swallowed in a single hoarse yell, answering the yell of the watchman who had been swaying half forgotten at his post in the foremast barrel. 'Seal-sign, sor – it's seal-sign! There's a Whitecoat off to port!'

Torrance was first to the side, and was almost knocked breathless by the following rush that drove him into the bulwark. There it was, a quarter of a mile off and already a little astern, a darker-white blob against a white patch of fresh-water ice. He turned with a single lunge, butted his way through the crowd, and wrenched a gaff from the rack beside the mizzenmast. Without a thought for his captain's dignity or for anything else, he found himself tumbling over the side, slithering across the floe. The month-old seal, a great-eyed, furry ball, lay whimpering beside the bobbing-hole through which its mother had just dived. It was as pitiful as ever, but it was the first of the fat. He was as hot and eager after it as he had been at seventeen, racing to his first kill.

He heard the shouts of his men behind him, laughing at him, cheering him on, and then, without conscious thought, he felt the change in the sound. The voices on his deck had deepened, there was anger in them now. There was a scrape of steps behind him, the breath of another runner, and a spatter of other shouts, more distant. He kept his eyes on the seal, for there was no need to look back. *Kestrel*, closed up to half a mile astern, had been as near to the sighting as he was.

The Whitecoat bawled before him, helpless and still blind, with the almost-human tears in the brown eyes. He was over it now, it had to be done quickly. It always had to with him; a man must think of the fat, not of the beast. The steel head of his gaff came down with smashing force, and just as it struck he felt the wind at his ear. Another gaff hurtled across his shoulder and nosed to the ice ahead, singing and shuddering. He spun round, hearing the roar from his deck, damning his own eyes that he had let it happen at all. He had been chasing his youth in the race, running from all that neared him, and it was closer than ever now.

Mahan walked past him, pulled the gaff from the ice, and turned back. He was grinning, sauntering now, hardly breathed by the run. As he paused by Torrance he looked down at the little mound of fur and blood lying between them and touched it with his foot, carelessly. 'No harm done, Robbie. Help yourself to the tail. Ye know I'd not have missed if I'd meant anything.'

'Do I?' He did know, but the sing of the passing gaff was still in his ear. He could hear the voices of his crew, and he could feel the silence in the ship that lay beyond them. 'Tell that to my lads over there. Tell it to your own.'

'Why? Have I made 'em a mite uneasy, d'ye think? It'll add spice to the hunt.' The head lifted, the lilt of the laugh came, and Mahan moved easily away, still with the silence waiting for him on his own deck. He passed deliberately under the ranks of glowering faces along *Jean Bright*'s bulwarks. Behind him a man spat, and a fresh-faced lad from the outports crossed himself stealthily. Torrance watched for a moment and bent to his work. He had lost the taste for it now, but the sooner over the better.

He hooked the wobbling body of the Whitecoat with his gaff and dragged it across the ice to the side of the ship. Johns had a whip broken out to lift it over, and the little fifty-pound carcase dropped on the deck with a thump. It had to be treated with ceremony, though it meant nothing. The Harp mother and the male who had dived for the bobbing-hole at the first smell of the ship had been one of the hermit couples. There would be others scattered about over hundreds of miles, and they were never the sign of a pack. Even so, and in spite of Mahan or the devil, there would still be the first drink to the first seal. All the more so now, Torrance thought, as he climbed over the side. The backslapping that met him was all forced and self-conscious; the men's eyes were dour with the thought of that whizzing spear.

He took out his knife while Johns and the four watchmasters gathered beside the Whitecoat with the whole crew circling them. One quick rip opened the underside of the pelt from nose to back flippers. Eben Gravely reached out for the flippers. They would come tonight, Torrance thought without enthusiasm, greasy and blackened by his arts to the captain's table. He cut off the small, bushy stub of the tail and stuffed it into his pocket. Peeling back the pelt with the three-inch layer of rubbery fat adhering to it, he dumped out the small ugly carcase. Then he cleaned the knife deliberately on the nearest proffered rag and stuck it back in his belt. 'Clear up the muck, lads, and then it's rum all round.' He turned below for the cabin with Johns and the watchmasters.

The special bottle came out of the cabin locker, and he set it on the table and filled his own glass. 'Tim's growing butter-fingered with that gaff.' He tried to make his voice light, but the lightness was not reflected in the hard faces round him. He lifted his glass, dipped the tail of the Whitecoat, and drank off the liquor. It was the turn of the mate next. Johns poured himself a drink that hovered over the rim, dipped the tail, sucked the drops adhering to the brush, and handed all to Hardy. Glass, bottle, and tail went round the circle of men and back to Torrance.

'Luck and log-loads.' They breathed the old, cheerful bless-ing.

Torrance put the bottle away and turned then to take down the dry wisp of last year's tail from the place where his father had wired it to the bulkhead. No thinking of that, he told him-self, but they were all thinking of it as he wired the other in place. The rite was over but they still stood, as if not knowing how to go.

'Ai-yeah.' Johns gave a windy breath, blowing away the mood or trying to. 'Now for the main patch.'

THE morning sun was gone as Torrance came up to the deck. By early afternoon the sky was grey lead and the ice was grey-black iron. The floe ridged and groaned ahead of the ship, wind-swept and bare. There were fewer channels, and they were more dangerous when they came. By the next dawn a crescent of saw-toothed bergs rode along the horizon, and all day there were no bobbing-holes, no seal-sign, nor any promise of it. The lone Whitecoat and the little patch of snow had been what they seemed, some aimless trick of instinct or accident of weather and wind. By nightfall the ship was nosing in among the bergs, stoking her fires lavishly in the search for ways around them. Then, toward midnight, came the feel of another change. The waxing moon broke through on a frosty glitter, and in the morning the ice ahead was patched with white.

It was hardly seal ice yet, but the promise, at least, was there, and it was high time. Johns was often below now, in the engine-room or the hold, and when he came up his silence was eloquent. The heavier going was eating away more coal. The mood of the men was settling into the old pattern. They had been lifted up for a while by the first sighting and the kill, but Mahan had dampened them down. The thought of that thrown gaff lingered with the smoke astern, sometimes ten miles back, sometimes closing to a mile, but always there, grimly, senselessly in their wake. There was more talk of the sombre morning on the ice, when word went round that Lije Torrance was nowhere to be found. The hunters and the deck-hands noted that the two captains who had come home last year with one of them flying the black flag and neither exchanging a signal were on the northward track again, and again in company. The bunkers were low again, the stokers added. There was something wrong with this voyage, and there was not much time to right it.

They were no new thing, Torrance told himself, these ups and downs in men as the long runs stretched out. But it helped no more than the sight of Johns's face. Little by little the ship's gloom seeped into him; he could feel himself giving way. His father had run the ship to her bunker's limits, but this was not last year. He was not his father, a man with his mind on his work. He was a man with a mind divided, smoke-blurred, thought-blurred, thinking of turning back.

It was the fifteenth day, and he had given himself another twenty hours when the sighting came. The ship was scunning easily through one of the rare patches of open water. He noticed a cluster of men gathering around the foremast, looking up at the barrelman. The man aloft was Hardy, standing with his feet braced and a telescope glued to his eye, swaying with the roll of the ship. The telescope did not come down, the arc of its sweep narrowed, and the crowd at the foot of the mast noticed it irritably.

'Ahoy there, Danny, ye scut!' The shouts began to go up. 'What the hell d'ye see? – what are ye playin' at? Will ye sing out?'

He waved them impatiently to silence, tense and irritable himself. The telescope swept away a little, swept back. Hardy was an old sealer with an old sealer's pride and pessimism; he would not speak till he was sure. But he was certainly interested. Torrance left his place by the wheel and joined the flow of men gathering beside the mast. The holds were emptying themselves onto the deck now, and the air was suddenly electric. 'Sign o' seals – sign o' seals!' – the word seemed to be running everywhere. Then, abruptly decisive, Hardy put down his telescope and leaned over to pick out Torrance below. 'It's something, sor – looks good. Dog, bitch, and Whitecoat, four miles on the starboard bow.'

The last of the off-watch men came flooding up, joining the crowd at the bulwarks, begging, trading, and wrestling for the few battered telescopes the ship possessed. 'She's a patch, sor –

112

sure of it!' The hail came down from the other barrel now, loudly affirmative. Then, as the ship drew to within a mile of the family, even before the dog and bitch slipped yapping into the water, the occasional bobbing-hole could be seen beyond them. Farther ahead more and more dark, broken blots appeared, always in clumps of three, the brown-backed mother and father beside the little hump of the Whitecoat, already lifting their heads, gazing in the direction of the ship with their ineffectual liquid brown eyes. *Jean Bright* was edging her way into the fringes of a patch, and it might well be the main patch.

Another hour would tell. With an abrupt impulse Torrance shouldered his way through the men at the foot of the mast and swung up to the barrel beside Hardy. The blots on the ice were growing along the horizon ahead, thickening. He could see beyond them the unbroken glitter of miles of fresh-water ice, seal ice. Every sign was right. He looked back to the south-west. Smoke as always, but it hung low. *Kestrel* had dropped well back in the night, farther than usual. She would have made no sighting yet. There were high bergs and long humps of ridging ice still ahead of her, masking this view. He swung a leg over the edge of the barrel, hooked his feet in the rope, and dropped to the deck again.

Johns was waiting for him, his pipe drawing evenly. As they moved away from the crowd of jostling men his eyes were quizzical. 'Well?'

'There's a lot of 'em. Too many for strays.'

'They're no strays. And the ice is right. You've done it, boy. I was beginning to have my doubts.'

'I've another of my own now.' Torrance hesitated, glanced astern. Johns's eyes followed. 'He'd be near twelve miles back, I'd say.'

'And a bit more. But he'll be pushing along soon. Always closes up before dark, specially when there's open water.'

'Aye.' Torrance nodded absently. He glanced off to port. Calm weather. A thirty-mile lane in the floe, miles wide in places, never narrower than a mile as far as he could see. Johns was looking at him speculatively. 'What's in your mind?'

'I'm thinking,' Torrance said slowly, 'we could maybe let

113

the patch wait a bit – if it is the patch. We could sheer off through that water there, carry on to the west for a bit, and then north. By nightfall, if the ice keeps open as it is, we could be fifty miles away.'

'With him on our tail still?'

'He'd follow. If we made a bit of extra smoke as we turned, he'd not wait to come up to this position. He'd not get a sighting at all. He'd break off from where he is now and cut after us. And he'd wake up in the morning fifty miles from the patch, with us gone. We'd work round him in the night, head back here all out, and get on with our business alone.'

Johns's glance was bleakly amused. 'Are ye serious?'

'Of course I'm serious!' Torrance bristled irritably. 'And why shouldn't I be? You'd the same idea yourself a few nights back.'

'That was earlier – and it was not much of an idea even then. Have ye thought what the lads would say now, after fifteen days of northing, if we turned away from the patch?'

'They'd guess what we were about. We could tell 'em, for that matter.'

'Aye.' Johns nodded with solemn irony. 'We could – or you could, for I'd not do it.'

'All right, then – out with it!' Torrance exploded angrily. 'You know what I'm up to and you don't like it. Why not?'

The old man knocked out his pipe, blew through it noisily, and began filling it again. 'In the first place he'd not cut away after us till he'd seen what made us change course. He'd come up through that muck back there and he'd find seal ice and seals. He'd go on – he'd be first into the patch.'

'All right – let him be. Let him fill up and get out. There's more already in sight than he could carry, and there's no other ship nearer than a hundred miles. We could stand off for a week and put back here when he's gone.'

'Without coal?'

Torrance stirred impatiently. 'We'd be hove-to most of the time. We'd not use much. It would be a close thing, but we could make it.'

Johns nodded absently. His pipe was drawing again. Then

114

he looked up, and there was a glint of tired humour warming the old eyes. 'You've always had the makings of a good captain, Robbie, and some of your father's ways. When Lije had a bad idea he'd try it on me – just to be sure. It'd not work. Ye want me to say that, don't ye? All right, I'll say it. You don't turn off from a patch when you've come for fat. You don't risk weather and ice. You've a crew that's on edge now, and they'd be out of hand in a week –'

'And?' Torrance looked over at him grimly as he paused.

'And you'd come back here and you'd find him still waiting.' The old voice hardened quietly. 'I say go for the patch.'

'All right.' Torrance straightened with a kind of relief. 'We stand on.'

The ship was groaning forward, and the jubilance of the men was rising with every turn of the screw. They were surely coming into the main patch. Thousands of the seal families scarred the ice about them and carpeted it to the horizon. *Jean Bright* was still cutting her way only through thickening fringes, but by nightfall she would be in the very heart of the great gathering of the beasts. By tomorrow sunrise there would be two hundred men on the ice, broken up into four hunting-watches, loaded down with gaffs and pan-flags and tow-ropes and sculping-knives. By sundown there would be five thousand Whitecoat pelts, each bubbling with its thick layer of fat, iced down in the holds or waiting in bloody mounds marked by the pan-flags. Tomorrow sundown – tomorrow night. Torrance looked back. The feather astern climbed and blew in the sunlight, the black hull beneath it came swaying and lunging on.

They were leaving the wide stretch of open water behind them but the polar pans rode loosely, real Harp ice now, covered with a thick white crust. The great cakes bobbed and crashed about the ship, slugging at its sides, but there was no wind and no swell. Lanes opened up easily before them as they bore inward, and the men hung over the bulwarks watching the change in the pack.

Hundreds of Whitecoats already left alone were bawling on the ice near at hand, and every thrust of the ship created new orphans. In the distance the brown Harps lifted their heads with

115

a thin clatter of dismay as the smell of the ship reached them. As the scent grew stronger they flopped to the holes in the ice and were instantly gone. Torrance felt the sick wave of distaste that always came with the sight, even more than from the crashing of gaffs and the clutter of blood and guts.

He was one of the men who would live out the next few days on bread and biscuit and tea, always with the heave of nausea threatening his middle. As a boy he had been ashamed of it, till he found that his father was like him, and many others. In as many more the hunt raised a ravenous hunger, but it seemed to be the same cause working both ways. Sealers loved the sea and the ice, and they loved the hunt, but they would have loved it better if the fat came as the cod came, in beaded blobs on the lines or vast, impersonal mounds in the bulging nets. Seals would not become the mere stuff of the sea; one watched them, watched their ways, thought of them and talked of them. While the pack lay undisturbed the parents fished for their infants and fed them on the ice, nursed them and cared for them with almost human tenderness. A mother Harp, the old men said, would disappear through her bobbing-hole, swim ten miles under the moving floe, and return by some marvellous instinct always to her own. Yet the instant men appeared, males and females dived from sight without a moment's hesitation and never returned.

The ship worked its way on cautiously and leisurely through the rest of the afternoon. She became a little lighter and a little trickier as the rock ballast went overboard in a splashing train astern. Even a few tons of the coal, so precious a day before, were tossed away with the rock. There was enough in the bunkers for the homeward trip, and there were pelts in sight for every inch of stowage. In a fog of coal dust and rock dust the carpenters and the helpers went at the stacks of timber on deck, knocking up pounds for the fat. By sunset the last baulks were in place, the last spikes home, and the deck was a checkerboard of bins, each with walls a foot thick and high as a man's chest. The holds below were the same, except that the pounds rose to the deckhead. They would be the first to be filled, and tomorrow night's sleepers would sleep on fat and ice, layered as high as their heads.

As dusk gathered, the ship lurched against a temporary cul-de-sac, with the wailing of the Whitecoats and the distant yapping of the Harps an unceasing chorus about her. A pull astern and then a smash ahead would set her free, but there was no need of it. She rested easily on the edge of a wide lake, five miles into the thickest area of the patch. It was far enough. Johns looked over at Torrance and Torrance shrugged. 'Burn her down.'

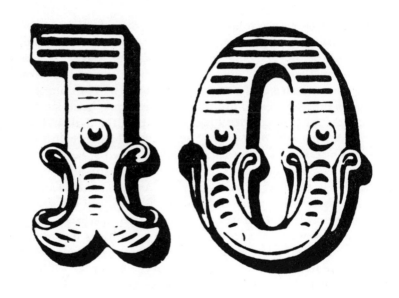

THE evening was foggy, but with full dark the light breeze wore round to the south of west. It was a clearing wind, and before morning the stars began to appear. It was going to be a good day. There was very little thought of sleep for anyone on board, and Torrance was glad of it. The clang and clatter of the men cleared his head, and their own heads seemed the clearer for it too. *Kestrel* had come up in the dark and lay burned down a mile or so away. She stood up blackly across the heave of water and ice, but hardly a man glanced at her.

On deck now the hands of the watch were listening to the noise below, eager to be making ready. As soon as the watches changed there was a great rush for the ladders, and the grindstones resumed their screaming as new men sharpened their knives. Those who had finished with the grindstones, or had not yet got to them, were greasing their boots, tightening loose cleats, bragging, and trading bets. From the galley, as a line of men pushed by him, Eben Gravely's voice rose in a hoarse, impersonal monotone. He was cursing out his clients as he filled their bread-sacks. It was all like every year, Torrance thought, all like the year before, and stopped himself there. The thought of Maura came, the other drumbeat began, and he fought it all off. Not now, not tonight. Listen to the racket, think of the men and the hunt, think of tomorrow and the fat.

He was still on deck, hardly aware that dawn was breaking, when the first scuffle of the rousing watches began. The clamour around the galley lifted again and began to fall as the breakfast was dished out. Perched on the sides of the pounds, squatted along the deck, wherever they could find a foot of space for their bottoms, men were clearing their pannikins of the salt pork and

119

the greasy biscuit, gulping their mugs of tea. The contents of a few of the pannikins went stealthily over the side, but the owners of the queasy stomachs were as quick as the others to sling their bread-sacks and take up their gaffs and tow-ropes. By full daylight the first watch was ready and waiting at the side. Hardy pointed to a pile of pan-flags and there was the usual bickering as to which half-dozen of the men should carry them. It was all quickly settled by the rough side of his tongue and a touch or two of his boot. The engines groaned softly as they worked up an easy head of steam, and before the ship got under way Hardy and his watch dropped overside onto the ice.

The fifty shouting men streamed off in a long file, then fanned out in sections. By the time they were a quarter-mile off they were in among the Whitecoats, laying about them with their gaffs. Torrance watched, sipping the mug of tea that Johns had brought along with his own. All distaste was gone now, or at least held down. This was the business of the voyage, this was the taking of the fat, as merciful as any of the takings of predatory man. A blow on the head or snout silenced each wailing infant. One man would kill from twenty to fifty Whitecoats in a day, thread the pelts on his tow-rope, and drag his load across the ice to where the master of the watch had set up a pan-flag. The piles of pelts would be heaved aboard by the whips as *Jean Bright* crawled with her skeleton crew of loaders among the pans and loose ice.

With the first watch away, the ship moved deeper into the patch to drop the second watch and then the third. The men behind her grew smaller in the distance, racing each other, leaping the six-foot gaps from pan to pan, their blood up with the killing, rejoicing in the freedom from the ship. Over a man's head the gaff point would wink for a moment, then come down. There would be the quick flash of the knife as it went for the quivering body, the yank of the skinning, the moment's wait while the pelt was threaded to the tow-rope, and the man would be moving again, his string lengthening behind him. Before dark the watches would have travelled miles over the floe and left their pan-flags behind them, whipping over mounds of pelts. The hunters would be tired and bloody and snapping at each other, with the seal fat and the seal red mingled noisomely on their faces and arms and bodies. Men who could eat nothing, and men who cut out the raw heart or liver from a beast they had just killed and gnawed at it ravenously. Working for the roof overhead, bread for the kin at home, they were not men to be played with.

The fourth watch went overside and the ship wore round. She was nearing the mounds of pelts already rising under Hardy's pan-flags, when the first watch from *Kestrel* filed onto the ice. The men passed under the bulwarks, fifty feet away, most of them with their heads down. Raw lads and the last scrapings from the outports, Johns had said, and it was true. They were a rough lot and a callow lot, sheep-faced and sulky now because they had sense enough at least to feel that something was wrong. The ice lay speckled with seals to the edge of every horizon; they could have been working a dozen miles away. Instead they would be side by side with touchy rivals, not a gaff's throw apart. It was quite clear from their faces that they would have been happier elsewhere, but they had their orders and they had the look of scared men.

They had hardly passed when the second watch came out, as ragged and seedy as the first, but with Mahan himself at the head of it. Johns stiffened, then stood solemnly watching with his pipe clamped in his mouth as the ship grated on ice and the file of men came streaming along by the bulwark. Mahan waved them on and paused, looking up at Torrance.

'Fine morning, Robbie.'

'It is that.'

'My lads and your lads and the ice under foot again.' He gestured around expansively. 'Ah, it's good to be here. D'ye not feel in the mood for a stroll yourself?'

'I do not.'

'Ah well, ye'd have Ernest glowering after ye, I expect.' He lifted his hand and turned with a little laugh. 'A Torrance must keep his place.'

Johns let out a sharp, explosive breath as he passed on. 'God damn him, he will let no chance go! His own fools are on edge and ours are watching 'em!'

'Let be, will you? You're getting edgy yourself.'

121

'I know the slob that he's got aboard as mate – flat-footed from dock-walking, booted from every schooner he ever sailed, and once before in the ice! If the Playfairs knew he'd left their ship with that scut – look at him!' He broke off, pointing angrily at Mahan and the men on the ice. 'He's setting that watch out side by side with ours – Hardy's yelling already!'

'Hardy can save his breath.' Torrance turned away from him as the ship neared a pan-flag. The whips swung out, the loaders followed them down, and the deck was sprayed with snowflakes, and slime, and blood, as the first bundles of pelts lurched upward and thumped aboard. There were more flags in the distance and the ship was soon abreast of them, soon on the move again. All over the ice the killing went on steadily, but the horseplay and laughter had begun to die out. A widening wave of silence had followed *Kestrel's* two last watches as they stumped after their mates. Uneasiness stole along, stalking all the watches, but there was no time to worry about it as the sun climbed toward noon and sloped away. The whips swung and dropped, the blubber went down through the hatches, and the inboard loaders slithered about in the holds, packing the first layers. By nightfall the mounds by fifty pan-flags had all been cleared away and were all growing again. *Jean Bright* reeked of fat, glistened with powdery ice, and her decks were awash with blood. The holds bubbled and gurgled as the heaving layers sank down, bedded in snow. There were four thousand pelts on board, Torrance guessed, and at least another two thousand waiting on the ice by the flags.

Yet for all the great day's killing the men came back at dusk moody and sullen. More of them than usual turned away from their food. Even the epicures who tossed flippers or hearts or livers to the cook sat in tired disinterest while the fires smoked in the galley. Eben Gravely and his three conscripted helpers did not dare deny the hands this privilege of the first day, but their work brought them no thanks. The meat was eaten when it came with the dull voracity of famished animals who were still troubled and alert. They were waiting, Torrance thought. He was waiting. Everything about the voyage, everything about this day, had taken on inexorably the shape of the year-long nightmare.

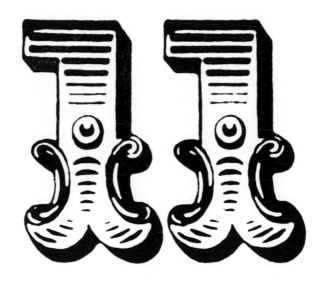

THE supper commotion died away in darkness, snuffed out by exhaustion. Even the galley clatter ended at last. Eben Gravely slept, wrapped in a blanket by his stove, and his helpers were sandwiched somewhere among their mates. Torrance could have slept standing, he had thought an hour before; he had moved through the fading bustle in a dim fog of weariness. Yet now with the new silence there was no closing his eyes. The stifling hush of his cabin had driven him back to the deck.

A full moon riding above the ice silhouetted the motionless ship a mile astern. Northern lights climbed jaggedly along the horizon, whispering up the sky in fangy arcs of blue, green, and yellow. Over the face of the floe, as it rocked southward with the current, the muted bawling of the seals was an incessant, eerie chorus. He stood bundled in his shapeless sea-gear, a taller patch of darkness breaking up the play of light and shadow on the checkered maze of the deck pounds. From beneath him and around him came the billowing snores of the men, sleeping the sleep of the dead. The half-dozen of the deck-watch yawned against the forward bulwark, out on their feet too. He was almost as alone in his wakefulness as any man could be, alone as Elijah Torrance the other night.

The thought would not let go. It marched through his head with the scrape of a dragged chain, fastened to every thought, rasping with new urgency. Tiredness crawled in his skin. His eyes ached with the shift of dazzle and darkness, yet he could not stop his peering. Five hundred miles of northing through the restless maze of the floe, and they had only led him back. He could not be fifty miles from last year's patch, the place where the thing had happened. He was here because of the seals, because of wind and weather, not by his own choice. Yet once again there were the pan-flags of two ships, side by side on the ice. Once again there was the vessel a mile away, that sombre blot in the moonlight, with the feather of vapour idling above its funnel.

He stiffened suddenly at the bulwark and relaxed with a soft oath. Once more he had half persuaded himself of the glimpse of a moving shadow, and once more he resisted the impulse to charge out after it. Formless wisps crawled everywhere across the gleaming face of the floe as the pans shifted. Now and then from the distance came the crash of a great berg riding down a lesser barrier. Everything that stirred held menace in this mood, in this place. The ice was a breeder of fancies as well as seals, a cold, miasmal fairyland where the thoughts of the healthiest head walked out in gruesome shapes.

There was a soft chunking of cleats along the deck, and Johns came out from the shadow of one of the pounds. He was keeping a watch on the captain, Torrance suspected, as much as on the ship. For a moment the two stood in silence, their eyes on the gloom and glitter of the floe. 'You've need of sleep,' Johns said gruffly at last.

'I know it. And it won't come.'

'Mahan.' The old man breathed the word with a shrug of flat acceptance and turned to lean on the bulwark. He was silent for a long moment, his eyes travelling the floe, fastening on the other ship. Then he spat deliberately, followed the spittle to the ice, and roused himself with an effort. 'I'll say it to ye just once more, boy, and then I'll hold my peace. Leave him alone.'

'You make it sound easy. Have your eyes been shut today? D'ye like the look of things now?'

'No. No, I don't.'

'And there's last year to think of. You've not forgot that either.'

'Nor the years before it, boy.' Johns turned to the bulwark and the silence lengthened again. Torrance studied the harsh planes of his face, softening in the moonlight. But he was still caught off guard when the words came at last, curiously and newly gentle. 'When did it all begin, Robbie? Was it the day the Portugee was killed?'

126

'What?' Torrance was lost for a moment, fumbling and bristling. 'What do you know about that?'

Johns merely nodded as if his question had been answered. 'We put that much together, Lije and I. You'd been there, you must have been. And a boy – seeing a thing like that –'

'I was a man,' Torrance said gruffly, 'when I saw Tim again. Or all but a man, anyway. It was near three years later. I'd time enough to get over it.'

'And Tim?'

'I'd not know. We've never spoken of it since.'

Johns nodded again. Something else was confirmed. 'Because ye do know. He'd not got over it – he never has. And there's no forgetting for you. The man he is, and the boy that was before – ye can't divide 'em, can you?'

Torrance shrugged, still shaken, struggling to recover himself. 'I'd not know. There's been too much else, Ernest. I'd a feeling for him once, yes – maybe I've never lost it, but –' he broke off, fretfully, fiercely, 'what would ye have me do? – what are ye trying to say? – d'ye forget all he's done?'

'None of it.' The old man drew a breath. 'Nor all that's been done to him. You've no part of it, and you still can't break free of it. Ye shut your eyes to it, and it still stares you in the face. I know.' He paused for a moment and glanced up again. 'Fifteen, the two of ye, when ye first shipped with Lije. I was standing with him by the gangway when ye walked up together. Four years in that ship, Robbie – you with Tim Mahan, and Lije and I watching. D'ye think we never spoke of it?'

'And what did ye say?' Torrance felt old horizons opening behind him. He wished them closed. A new coldness and tiredness seemed to run the length of his body.

'Lije blamed himself. He'd let ye run too freely with a brat of Kevin Mahan's, son or not – born of the scum – bred to it –'

'No!' The word broke from Torrance, agonized, almost a shout. 'He would not say that – he could not! Born of the scum and bred to it – fine, fat, comfortable words! And they set him off from the rest of us, did they – made him of no account?'

Johns nodded doggedly. 'He said it, Robbie – and I said it. In all the clean-washed pride of us – in our good luck – in the safe, fat lives that were not to be shared with his like. Give a

127

little and he'd take all – share a little and ye'd share what was laid on him. The weight of all that filth – Dogstown and Kevin Mahan and the whore that mothered him – it was all laid on the boy, and it was too much – it was not for us. He carried it, and we would not. So we sent him away – the scapegoat.'

'Scapegoat?'

Johns nodded, fumbling for his pipe and forgetting it, his face working in the moonlight. 'Aye. Sent him away from the clean men and the clean ship, with his filth on him. I watched him go down the gangway and it felt good. It felt light. But he was not gone, was he? He would not go. He was there with you in your life and then it was Maura's life, and they were both more to Lije than his own had ever been, but – still there was the thought of the lad he'd sent away.'

'How d'ye know all this?' Torrance said huskily. 'He never spoke of it to me.'

'Nor to me. Not so long as he lived. But there was no need of it, for I knew. And the words were there behind him.'

'What?'

Johns was silent for a moment, following the play of the wild greens and yellows dancing along the horizon. Then his voice came, strangely. ' "And Aaron shall lay both hands upon the head of the live goat and confess over him all the iniquities of the children of Israel and all their transgressions in all their sins, putting them upon the head of the goat. And the goat shall bear upon him all their iniquities unto a land not inhabited." ' He was still looking out from the bulwark. The words flowed familiarly from somewhere deep in his mind, long carved there, long pondered, yet curiously hard and biting. Torrance stiffened away from him.

'What the devil would that be? – Scripture?'

'Leviticus 16,' Johns said flatly, dryly. 'The book o' the scapegoat. The morning Lije was gone I went down to look for him in his cabin. His Bible was open on his desk with the verses marked in it. Long marked, with the pencil lines near rubbed out. He'd conned that passage for years, boy. He'd lived with it and suffered with it. It spoke of what he'd done to Mahan.'

'Fancies – rubbish!' Torrance was shaken and angry. 'How could ye know that?'

128

'Fancies if ye like.' Johns shrugged. 'But I knew Lije and I know myself. He read those words and they made him part of the rest – of all that was laid on the boy. They were cruel as stone and they lay on him like stone – they kept his hand from Mahan for a dozen years. But there was the thought of you too, and it got to be too much. The words failed him that night. He left the book behind him and he came up on the deck. And he went out to the ice to do what he could not do. Nor you either, Robbie. You'll leave Mahan to himself.'

'So that's what you've kept in the back of your head for a year.' Torrance's voice was hoarse; he was reaching for gruff scorn. 'It's not much. He did not go out because of a scrap of scripture. He went out because of me. It's been my thought, and it's yours. I know that now, at least.'

'And ye feel the lighter for it, boy?' The old man turned on him with soft, probing intentness. 'Why do ye watch that ship? Why do ye stand here now with your legs rubber beneath ye, drunk with tiredness? Waiting for Mahan? – you could not lift a hand to him. You've reached too deep in his heart, boy, you've carried the weight too long. And you'll have to live with it still, for there's no shaking it off!'

Torrance straightened at the bulwark, struck it softly with his hand. 'If it's pity you're talking of, Ernest, he's long past it now. And it's not that he wants. It'll be one of us or the other.'

'No.' Johns straightened with him as the watch-bell struck from amidships. 'You'll hold onto yourself for a few more days. You'll get your ship safe home. And for him – there's only the one way now, the one place – leave him to come to it.' His voice had softened. He was looking away from Torrance over the moonlit, frozen vastness, teeming with the sounds that seemed to deepen silence. 'Here. I'd not know how or when, but it'll be here. "A land not inhabited . . ." '

He broke off. Torrance was no longer listening. He was leaning out from the bulwark, searching the shadows of the floe. There had been a sound there, sharp amid other sounds, the clink of a gaff on ice. It came again. Johns's fingers closed on his arm, gripping it, turning him.

'If ye go out there, I go with you.'

He flung off the hand and swung himself to the bulwark,

then stopped. Huge and overpowering, the wave of his gathered weariness flooded over him. 'All right. We'll have it your
way.' He dropped to the deck again, turned his back on the ice,
and made for the cabin ladder.

Stretched out on his bunk in darkness, he listened to the
watch-bell measuring away the night. Half a dozen times he
started up and sank back as the ship sounds and the ice sounds
and the welter of tense imaginings seethed and blurred. Slowly
they became a whole, gripping him and numbing him, sucking
him down in sleep. When he started awake, a ray of morning
sunlight was creeping along the bulkhead. Johns stood in the
doorway, his face a hard mask.

'First watch out on the ice already. Was going to let you
sleep till we got under way.'

'Well?'

'Can't wait for it now. You'd better come up.'

'Trouble?' Torrance was already into his boots, reaching
for his cap and jacket.

'Aye.' The face was still expressionless. 'Half a dozen pan-
flags been shifted in the night.'

Torrance kept his head down, busied his hands with the
jacket. He did not want to show the surge of relief, the stony,
exultant quiet. But Johns stood squarely in front of him as he
started through the doorway. 'Wait a minute.'

'Well?'

'Have ye thought beyond yourself? A fight between ships
in the ice could mean the end of the lot of us.'

'There'll be no fight between ships.' He brushed past, clattered up the companion-ladder, and shoved his way through a
crowd of angry men. His face was as blank as Johns's had been,
and for the first time in a year he was deadly sure of himself. For
the first time since the sailing-day in St. John's he was glad he
had made the voyage. Maura and Johns had been right for whatever reason. There was no turning away.

As he came to the quarter-deck bulwark, he could see the
men of the first hunting-watch. They were milling about among
pan-flags half a mile away, and with them was the first watch
from *Kestrel*. There were eighty or ninety men, broken into

ragged groups, each about a mound of pelts. By now they should have been deep into the floe, relaxed and confident with a good day's work behind them, racing each other across the pans, trading jovial insults. Instead, they were shuffling with cocked fists and an air of furious mystification around the piles they had left last night. Even from the ship the dangerous electricity could be felt, and it had already communicated itself to the men of the other three watches.

Kestrel had steam up, but she gave no sign of moving. Her bulwarks were lined too. He could see the heads swivel, following Hardy, as the watchmaster broke away from the crowd on the ice and stumped purposefully through the sish toward *Jean Bright*. Hardy's mood was plain in every muscle, and as he came in under the loom of the side he looked up at Torrance with a scowl black beneath his two weeks' crop of stubble. 'Ye'd better come out here. There's *Kestrel* flags been set onto our piles – I've counted eight for sure. Near a thousand pelts stolen.'

Torrance was still studying the groups about the pan-flags. Mahan was not on the ice. 'What do the *Kestrel* lads say?'

'Say they know nothing about it. And they'll not give up a pelt under their flags.'

'No more would you. And there's no proving anything now.'

Hardy's anger flared up. 'You know who's done it! And so do I!' He gestured furiously in the direction of *Kestrel*. 'It's happened before to ships lying near him.'

'I say there's no proving it. Two hours' work will make up the pelts we've lost, if we've lost any. Leave all as it is, and set up new flags.'

'What!'

'Leave all as it is, I say, and get on with the killing.'

'The men'll not go!'

'You'll tell 'em it's my orders and you'll see they go! Or I get a new watchmaster.'

Hardy gave him a long, baffled stare, shook his head, and started back across the ice. Torrance watched as he reached the men by the pan-flags. The groups came together, surged with debate for a while, and then divided again, streaming away in

131

their files, separate and sullen. On deck the startled flare of out-rage was dying away too, but the silence was not reassuring. He swung round, pushed through the crowd of gaping, muttering men, and came up to Ernest Johns. 'Get under way.'

The engine telegraph clanged, and the ship shuddered away under an easy head of steam. Bumping along and pausing in the jagged aisles of the floe, it dropped the three remaining watches one by one. As the last men cleared the side, sharp-tempered and edgy, *Jean Bright* wore round to turn in open water and move back to the flags for loading. *Kestrel's* fourth watch was just going over. Both ships would be down now to skeleton crews of ship-handlers and loaders. Torrance selected a gaff from the rack against the bulkhead and turned to Johns. 'Wear up to the ice there, near to where she's lying. You'll take over for a bit.'

Johns stiffened, hesitated for a moment, then turned and gave the order to the helmsman. As the ship came round he was silent, watching the hunters receding into the floe. Protest was eloquent in every line of his body, and his voice was harsh when he spoke. 'You've acted like a captain so far. Now you're a fool.'

'Is he to be let go on with it?'

'We're in a rich patch. A few pelts either way is no matter. And it's not the pelts you're thinking of.'

'Maybe it's not. I'm thinking there'll be more flags changed tonight – and more the next night – till we've four hundred men at each other's throats.'

'Robbie –'

'Wear up, I say.'

The ship's side grated against the ice, a quarter of a mile from *Kestrel*. Torrance swung over the bulwark, dropped down to the floe, and stood for a moment studying ice and sky. 'Get on with the loading. If the wind works round to the north-west we'll be in for thick weather. Don't wait too long to call the men in.'

Johns nodded. His eyes were sombre, and the lines stood clear and deep in the fresh, wind-burned face. Some time during the night or the early morning he had taken the fancy to shave. It was a way of his; he had known the spanking decks of the old square-riggers, and the habits of cleanly ships persisted in the ice. Or he had shaved to pass the time; he had not slept much. 'Do it, then – and be sure you're man enough.' His voice had hardened to the grey coldness of the polar ice. 'For you've no choice now.'

THE nearest men on the ice were looking back, curious at the doings on the ship. Torrance turned away from them deliberately and moved along by the hull till the curve of the waist hid him. He could still be seen from the deck, but there were not many to watch and Johns would keep them busy. *Kestrel* lay broadside on to him and stopped, across a clear, level expanse already emptied of Whitecoats. He started for her, feeling the ice strange to his feet after seventeen days at sea, reaching ahead with his gaff to probe the sish that looked like solid ice but lay, a yielding film, above open water. The sun still cast a dazzling glare on the floe, but the mood of the day was changing. He could feel the uneasiness of the weather and smell snow riding far off in the wind.

He was within a hundred yards of *Kestrel* when he looked up and paused. There was a figure separating from the loom of the ship's side. Mahan had seen him coming and had slipped onto the ice. But he was not advancing to meet him. Gaff in hand, moving with elaborate casualness, he was heading off into the floe, away from the hunting-watches.

It would be better this way. Torrance lounged along till Mahan had put about a quarter of a mile between them and then began to follow, matching the other's air of unconcern. Sooner or later one of the hummocks where the ice had rafted would hide the two captains from their crews.

They went on for half an hour and then Mahan bore off leisurely toward the foot of a broad, jagged ridge where wind and swell had lifted the pans one on top of another to a height of nearly thirty feet. He climbed the ridge, straightened along the skyline, and then, without a backward look, disappeared

135

down the other side. As Torrance reached the top and picked his way forward among the saw-toothed blocks of the crest, he stopped for a moment. He could take in the view below from here, and he did not like the look of it.

Mahan was resting on his haunches at the edge of a small lake of black water. Running out from the edge was a narrow neck of ice, joining with a pan forty or fifty feet square in the middle of the lake. The pan must have drifted in through a channel that was now closed, and riding on it had come a pair of Hoods, the warrior seals who travelled among the Harps, always aloof and dangerous. These two were full-grown, already disturbed and watchful. The grey bodies were lifting a little on the powerful flippers, the tough, furred helmets that gave the beasts their name were beginning to distend. Around the lake and beyond it the ice lay white and empty. There was a curious kind of silence. There were no sealers and no seals; the Harps avoided the Hoods. Torrance felt a cool, warning tremor run through his muscles. Mahan had known the Hoods were here, and had chosen the place deliberately.

He watched, still squatting, as Torrance began to pick his way down the slope. Then, as the other neared him across the rough glare-ice by the water, Mahan stood up. The cap sat back on his head as carelessly as ever. The stray black lock coiled down below the peak. The jacket collar was open, and the sun-burned throat rose out of it, beautiful as always, but the restless eyes seemed set deeper in his head. Even that face wore the mark of the seventeen days. He took a step or two forward, lithely testing the footing. Then he waited, the gaff slung easily in his hand. Tall and alone, with the black water behind him and the wildness of the ice about him, he seemed at home in this place, a part of it. 'A land not inhabited.' Torrance wrenched his mind away from the thought.

'Well, Robbie?' They were facing each other, six feet apart, amid the strewn humps of the ice-blocks, with the sun glinting on the slippery shoreline. The voice was as soft and wandering and light as ever. 'You wanted a word with me.'

'I did. I'm here to tell you you've changed your last pan-flag.'

136

'Ah.' The trifle seemed to amuse him. 'And who says I've done such a thing?'

'You've two choices. You'll come back with me this instant, before the loaders get to 'em, and take down the flags you shifted last night.'

'That's one.'

'Or you'll call your watches in. You'll load what's under your flags, our pelts or not – I'll give you what you've stolen. But you'll be off from here by dusk to the far side of the patch, and you'll not commence tomorrow till you're a good ten miles off.'

'That'd be the second choice. There's a good, familiar ring to 'em, Robbie lad. I was offered both last year – did ye not guess it?'

'I did. But it's not the dark of the night now, and it's not an old man. One or the other, Tim – or we settle our business here.'

'Our business.' Mahan nodded to the words, but he was barely listening. There was no change in the intent stillness of the poised body. The smile came, growing from nothing still, always from nothing. 'Pan-flags and fat – now what the hell's all that to either of us? – what's it ever been? Or to Lije Torrance? D'ye think the old man cared for a pile of pelts?'

The mockery was insistent, maddening. Torrance could feel the quickening of his breath, the wave of bitter anguish smashing at the last of his dikes. 'Ye were shifting pan-flags half a mile from the ship. My father knew what ye were up to, and he knew why. He was seventy-one years old – he should have roused the watch. But he didn't – he came out to you himself –'

'With his last chances.' The irony was deadlier now. 'Get out o' the patch, or he'd raise a shout for the watch. Give up my berth when we got back to St. John's. Get off the island – out of his dear son's life. Set off again, the Jinker without a ship, and the name trailing behind me, to tramp docks on the mainland. Ah, they were good, Robbie, those last chances of his.'

'And then what?' Torrance lashed at the smile, savagely. 'Did he turn his back on ye, Tim? Did he look away for a minute? Ye let him have it with a gaff or a knife. Ye shoved his body into a crack in the floe, and ye crawled back to your ship!'

137

It was out now. He waited, hoping for the sudden spring that would release the gaff itching in his hand. But Mahan merely shrugged. The black eyes strayed away from him and came back, careless and glinting. 'Aye. That was the way of it, more or less. That was the end of Lije. But is that all ye came out to talk of, Robbie? Nothing more than that?'

'More!' The cry rose and broke. The soft laugh came over it.

'Too much more. No saying it all, is there? The old man went in his time, Robbie, for he'd cluttered the way too long. He'd have done better to boot me off his ship the day I came aboard of it, fifteen years old. He wanted to – ye know that well enough.'

'Aye, I do. And he was right! It was my doing kept you there.'

'So it was. Through the four years of it. Side by side in the 'tween decks, listening to each other's snores. Standing the watches together, north and south, hunting out new mischief. Ah, they were good enough days, Robbie, till he put an end to 'em. Not a lad to his taste, was I – with Dogstown and all behind me?'

'Let be with that. It's gone.' Torrance's voice was husky. But the other watched him, measuring and knowing still. The eyes lingered and played with him, biding their own time. The hands were relaxed on the gaff, the voice came even and amused.

'D'ye remember that time in the ice, our first run – and us by the flag and the pile of pelts I'd shifted? It was you and me to-gether then, solid as steel – and you, blustering and red, holding to your first lie – full in your father's face. Now why would ye do that, Robbie?'

Torrance said nothing. His father's face, he must keep that face before him. Yet the voice seemed to twine around him, tie him, drain him.

'And the nights ashore in the south – always together. Al-most always. Till ye got restless. Ye were snappish with me, I remember, as we came into Malaga. Ah Malaga – ye'll remember the whore in Malaga?'

There was a new thrust in the words, and Torrance stiff-ened. The black eyes glittered snakily, holding him fast. The far-off night was in them, rancid with sour wine, heavy with sweaty scent. A scared young oaf was leaping back from a bed, pantlegs tangling his ankles, staring at the burst-in door. He could see the knife again, and the face above it. It had been the face of the boy that Dogstown afternoon; the boy Tim's eyes had glared from that twisted mask, savage with new loss. There had been gross, white-curving nakedness, there had been tangled hair and blood, blood like the blood that had stained the Dogstown bed, screams like those screams. He had thought of it all, sickened with it all again as the woman shrilled behind him and he fought the knife away from her, stumbling and ludicrous, sheltering her body with his own, grabbing at the hand that drove the steel for the flesh, glaring at the wild eyes. The eyes still glared, the wildness lying deep. The voice went wheedling on.

'Now what would you be doing with a slut like that, Robbie? Ye were a boy. She'd have had your wallet from you and sent you off with another sort of packet. That's why I broke it up.'

'Was it?' Torrance looked out across the ridges of the floe, away from the eyes. His voice came dull and flat, heavy as the bond he had tried to break that night, looking for denial even in the stews of the port, even in that nauseous bed. 'Ye broke it up because she was a woman, Tim, and because you're what you are. I think my father knew it from that night on. And I knew.' He flared suddenly, his voice loud, hearing the whimpering cries, seeing the twin obscenities of the gashed breasts. 'And ye were too much – too much for a man to bear with even then!'

'Was I now? And what d'ye mean by that, Robbie? Let's have it out at last.'

'I should have been rid of ye for good and all! It should have been the end when ye walked down the gangway. And it would have been, if I'd not known what made you!'

'Made me?' There was a quick new curiosity, a sudden change in the tone.

'But I do know – I saw it – it's as though I'd had a hand in it. You've been a curse and a madman ever since that day!'

'What day?'

139

The question came, innocent and alert, stopping Torrance for a moment, teasing him still, he thought. Mahan's smile was back in place, but the eyes were steadier on him. There might have been real puzzlement in them, there might have been a hint of fear. He brushed it aside, impatiently. 'I stood too much because of it, I tried to forgive too much. The more fool me.'

'What's this day you're talking of?' The question came again, sharper, more pressing, cutting across his words.

'You've no need to be told of it, and I've no mind for the telling.' Torrance fumbled and shied, blocking away the memory. 'But it changed you. We were boys and friends once – you were never a boy again.'

'I said – what day?' The words snapped out at him now like a cracked whip, and Torrance felt his fingers tighten on the gaff. But Mahan had made no move. He was standing utterly still, with only a new paleness under the olive skin. The voice had lost its lilt; it was husky now. 'I asked ye what did ye see, Robbie – and when?'

Torrance gaped at him, fully stopped now. An unimaginable doubt was groping forward. The question was meant; there was something real pleading in those eyes for once. The voice came, straining this time for lightness.

'What would it be now, Robbie, this great thing?'

Torrance could feel the strain, the fear beneath the shaken insistence. His own voice was husky now, tightening in his dry throat. 'I'm talking of the day in Dogstown – when we came to your house together. Why do ye play with me?'

'Dogstown? As a boy?' Mahan threw back his head, and the sudden laugh was loud, genuine with relief and ridicule. 'What are ye talking of? – ye've been nursing some boy's fancy. A goodly, godly Torrance in Kevin Mahan's house? Now that'd be a thing to think of, wouldn't it?'

'I was there, I tell you! We were both there together.' Some brink was opening that Torrance had never dreamed of. Amid his anger and his urgency he felt a sick, cold dismay. But he pressed on; he could not stop himself now. 'It was the day we spilled in the dory.'

He seemed to have made no impression. Mahan waved the

140

words away, still with the laugh. 'Dories we may have spilled in, for all I know – we were out in 'em enough, but –'

'Grogan's dory!' – Torrance was still pressing, shaken, yet driven on. 'We'd stolen it from the wharf at Maggoty Cove – we were out by the rocks, Tim – and I dropped an oar and went after it, and you fished me out and –'

He broke off. The sound had been hardly a sigh, but behind the black eyes there was a growth like merciless light. Mahan put up a hand, mutely, helplessly, as though warding away the beam. Then the hand came down, limply. 'And ye stood there in your wet togs with the door opening as we came up to it,' – Mahan's voice was hardly his own, he was not hearing the words, he did not know he was speaking – 'and he was crawling out with his back sagging like a worm – and it was Kevin over her inside, and she there on the bed, and –'

He looked up, seeing everything and seeing nothing. The boy's eyes stared from the man's face. It seemed to Torrance that the wild, shrill cry of the boy rang in his ears. Yet there had been no sound; there was only the blind, white silence and the flood of linking warmth. He heard the clatter of the falling gaff. He dropped his own and was reaching out with his hands; he was too late. Mahan had dissolved before him in a single movement, he was a settling hump on the ice. In the man's face, glistening with beaded sweat, the eyes of the boy were blank to the world around him, staring inward.

IT was like a tearing loose of wreckage in the depths, a wrenching swirl in blackness, the sudden grip of power, infinite and cold, forcing him upward into leaden light. On the old sea-tracks to the south he had seen them often, black timbers, fragments of forgotten ships, barely awash, heavy with slime, crusted with growth and death. Freed to a second death, he had thought, watching them, brooding on them, always alone whatever deck he stood on. Loneliness ultimate and unrelieved; something in him held kinship with those fragments. He had imagined the stir of their going far beneath, the stealthy crack rippling the blind sea-floor, the heave of sand, the suck of slime and weeds, the darting swarms of fish, eyeless, deformed by depth, startling away. The long upward passage to relentless light, to merciless resurrection; he had imagined that too. Now he was living it.

The face swirled with him rising from the depths, took shape; the voice came. He saw the rose in her hair, that summer rose from the hills, sun-starved, sand-blown, hardy and defiant as the rocks it grew on. Each summer day she had gone to the hills for a rose; he had gone himself for her as he grew older. The island tang in her voice, the island blue in her eyes, the ways of the waterfront; she had been native enough and rough enough, that Rose. Rose; yes, it was her name, a rum-thick snarl on the lips of Kevin Mahan. Kevin – the stink of the lanes and grog shops filled his nostrils, he felt the fist and the boot, the bruises purpled again.

Rose – Rosa – the name was sudden in the other voice, urgent and soft. The white teeth flashed in the brown face, the smile broke, warming the wonder of those rare, swift days. The

143

days of the Portugee; a dozen days in all the years of the boy, and yet they had lived for them, Rose and the boy. For her the ritual of the rose was promise and remembrance, he had known that. Defiance too; he had sensed that too, and known that Kevin sensed it. He had feared for her and envied her her strength, flaunting that reckless challenge, waiting for the next day.

Each spring had brought the cluster of sail from the south, glimpsed from a hill-top, riding away in mist, rising again and fading. The brown-faced smiling men from the warmer seas were north again for the cod. There would be the green on the slopes, the rose in her hair, the wakening and the waiting. Day-long, summer-long, on to the autumn gales, the fleet would circle the island. The weeks would come that emptied the house of Kevin, off for a trick as deck-hand or a stint with a Banker's dory. Often the weeks were empty as the house, sluttish and blank and sullen as the house. The Portugees put in for their day ashore. The bright scarves flecked the docks, but no one came. She gave no sign of hope or disappointment. She could have known nothing of the ships or men; no messenger came to whisper in the lane. Often, if she looked, it was Kevin she saw instead, back with his pay gone, parched and raw with drink, savage at the thought of walking docks again.

Yet there were other days with Kevin gone. Even at the promised going the change would come. Lightness would rise in her and reach the boy. There would be fear and hope, expectancy and stealth running like a current through them, lifting both. He would share the midnights and the fears with her, counting the hoarded pennies, hiding the cakes. He would watch her mending the frock while Kevin slept, the one good frock, the frock for the one day. Sensing her wakening body he would fear that Kevin sensed it. He would hold his breath with her while the slung sea-bag and the hulking shoulders passed through the sagging doorway. He would follow them along the twisting paths to the dock, see them aboard the ship, watch till the mast-tips wavered out of harbour, loving the lightness that that going brought. Then he would run back to the time of the other waiting.

Whether it would be weeks or days he never knew, never

cared. He was sure in her strange sureness, changing with her change. He would know the miracle of the swept hearth, the glowing coal-fire, the blue dress like a summer sky afloat under the harsh red hair. He would watch the harshness soften, rippling under the brush, shaped to the glowing coil, crowned by the rose. He would see her lips, softening too and parted, as the knock came at the door and waiting ended. There would be the other form in the doorway, the flare of the bright scarf, the glint of the gold ear-ring, the laugh like alien music. There would be the strange words, strange as a caress, the dusty bottle, and the clutch of wind-blown roses out-thrust in the brown hands. The hands would lift him laughing from the floor, dangling the bag of sweets.

Sent off then to be gone while the strange, mucky necessities of man and woman were dealt with, he would come home always to the dying coals, the tossed bed, the litter of crumbs and glasses sticky with their red lees. Yet always to the plate aside piled high for himself, the drop of wine, the place by the dying fire, the brown hand on his head. Welcomed and one with them he would share the hour, watching the fire die. The sated bodies drew together still, hands linked around him, and the day was over. Yet it had been; its warmth was warm in him. It was enough, all that he asked or knew of, this and the promise of another day, promising no more. There would be stealth again, warnings again, waiting again. Flowers and fire would go with the emptied bottle, the blue dress vanish deep in the mouldering chest. The film would crawl again over the slow months, smearing the crazy table, dirtying the cracked floor. Driftwood would smoulder stinking on the hearth, the glowing hair grow drab and harsh again, trapped in the sluttish knot. All things would settle, withering, into the grey hell made by Kevin, yet still there would be beyond it the promise of the flaunting rose, the promise of the next day.

She asked no more and thought no more for herself. Her care for the boy stopped short at one hard purpose. 'You will have schooling,' she said in the flat, harsh voice. 'There will be no getting away from him without it – you would be another like him.' She knew no other reason and needed none; that was

145

enough for both. Smelling of Dogstown, jeered at in Dogstown lanes, always the outcast when he went beyond them, he climbed the road to the school.

What he felt for her he could not say. His lips had never known the shape of the word. He had never known the name of the Portugee. Why she had churched with Kevin – if she had churched with him – the questions never came. A girl of the waterfront hovels; something like Kevin had always been her fate, accepted with a shrug. There had been men enough beside him; it did not occur to the boy to question that. There was one now, one only; this was unquestioned too, the base of his life. Somewhere, at some time, on some squalid tavern mattress or the grass by some reeking lane, there had been this flowering from the mud. She loved the Portugee and loved his child.

The rose in the hair, the face, the touch of the hand; they had lain in blackness under the twenty years. Plunged down and now plucked up by infinite power, merciless and hostile still. That thumb had pressed the darkness into his temples, those shapes had stirred and groped. They had beaten at bars and could not be set free; he had known he dared not free them if he could. Better to let them settle in the depths, restless and cold and overwashed by years; better to build the man anew from fragments. They had come to him month by month and year by year, those cloudy scraps that drifted up from the dark, always with greater darkness lying deep. They had haunted the watches, walked in the dock-side streets, risen in the white, cold desert of the ice. Comfortless always, always without form. The reek of Dogstown and the curse of boyhood, Kevin, his woman, and his woman's man; they had been shapes and husks and fading glimpses, mingled in half-light, blurred and blotted out. The names had circled round a core of blackness, wearing no faces, never finding voice. They were of him, they had made him, they were gone. The man was here, the boyhood somehow ended. The smell of filth remained.

Robbie. The boy's face unforgotten, changed to the man's. Changed with that changing he had never fathomed. The school-yard days, the days on the docks and hills, crowded, confused, and waveringly bright; they had always stopped short at that

146

broad scar of darkness. That darkness giving now to merciless light. The dory lashing in the oily sea, terror and sudden lightness, soaring pride. The young voice rose in his throat warmed with the pride, the wet boots sloshed through pounding rain to the door. The door; the door opened –

Daylight about him and a glint of sun. He felt the cold of the ice; his body stirred. He heard his own voice, a little choking moan. Rose – the red hair flowed tangled over her back, matted with shreds of blue. Rose – the black belt came down, the skin tore bubbling red, tore with that sound. Rose! – Robbie! – the cry broke from his throat. Her arms were round him, comforting the boy. Her hands –

They were hard hands, hard and scarred, yet in this moment gentle. They raised him, limp and swaying, and drew off. He looked up slowly, knowing what he would see, wanting their touch still.

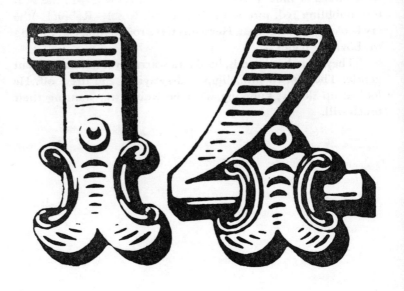

THE gaffs lay on the ice. Torrance bent down to his own and straightened with it slowly. Ten minutes, perhaps – he had lost all count of time. Ten minutes, standing in sunlight over the huddled hump, watching the stir of limbs, the beaded face. Fathomless change, changing him too. The gaff drooped in his hands.

Mahan had settled onto a block of ice. He sat there, hands between his parted knees, head down. Fathomless change, changing nothing. There was still no end, and the end would have to come. Not now, not yet. Torrance moved across to the other gaff, kicked it over to rattle against Mahan's boot. 'You're all right now.' He made his voice flat and hard. 'We'll go back and set new flags.'

'No, we'll not.' Mahan reached down and picked up the gaff but made no other move. The voice was as flat as Torrance's, the lilt gone out of it. 'Ye've laid me open to the backbone like a split fish. I'd like to look for a bit.'

'I did not know –' Torrance began huskily. 'I'd not have brought it all back to you, if –'

'But ye did.' Mahan cut him off indifferently. 'And no thanks to you.' He was silent for a moment and then straightened a little, drawing a long breath. 'So that was the way of it. The one woman I could ever bear the sight of. No good, but she was good to me – the one thing. The one thing, Robbie, that tied me in to my kind, made me something more than the dogs and rats in the street. It was her going, I expect – going like that –' He paused, looked up briefly. 'She was dead, was she, when Kevin had finished with her?'

'No. Not then.'

'Ye'd not know how she came to her end when she did?'

'No.'

Mahan looked down again. The muscles of his throat worked. 'No matter. She was dead all right that day, breathing or not.' His hands rose for a moment, settled back. Then he looked up and his eyes steadied on Torrance's face, quizzical and musing. 'And you'd seen the whole of it. It always lay there, alive in your eyes when you looked at me. I did not know what to make of it. All gone –' He paused again, mulling it over, it seemed, groping incredulously through a whirling welter. 'D'ye know where I came to myself, Robbie – if ye can call it that?'

'No.'

'I woke up on a schooner bound for Spain – three days out. It seemed an odd business and I was troubled enough for a while. My head ached like the devil and I was sick and scared and miserable. But after all, there was nothing so strange about it. I was a lad on shipboard – I'd run away to sea. God knows I'd thought of it enough – I remembered that.'

Torrance nodded. What boy had not thought of it? The thoughts of the boys swarmed round him for a moment; he fought them away. Mahan was not looking at him. He was still unravelling the strands, meditative, absorbed. He shook his head with a little wondering laugh. 'In a week I was at home in the ship, thinking nothing of it. Though how I'd got there – what I'd done – it nagged at me for a bit, scared me. To tell you the truth, I got in the way of thinking I'd killed Kevin – there was a lad aboard that knew him and he talked of him sometimes, and there were scraps and bits came back to me – the feel of him, anyway. I'd wanted to kill him – maybe I had – I was afraid to ask. D'ye believe all this?'

'Why should ye lie to me now?' Torrance settled beside him on the ice block, heavily. That numbing sleep of nearness held him still. Those hands had killed his father. Those hands – he would not think of the rest. For all the hate, all the grief, all the waste and bitterness of the maimed life, there was still that deadly kinship. The tangling burden clung like the weight of the world. He must carry it back to the ship, carry it on. He did not know how he could.

150

Mahan let the gaff handle settle between his knees, watching it moodily. 'When pay-time came in Cadiz, they showed me my papers. I'd walked aboard in St. John's all right, and signed up like a man. And yet with all the telling there was not a bit came back to me. Nothing. Never till this day. So I went on to another schooner and another after that, with three days of blackness always lurking behind me. I thought about 'em, all right. I'd lie in my bunk rummaging round in that blackness, finding nothing. Then I gave up. Whatever it was, it was done with.'

They sat for a moment quietly, side by side, looking at the water, and the ice, and the restless Hoods. Then, like the sounding of a thin, warning chord, came the sense of another mood. Torrance turned and found Mahan's eyes on him, black and deep, troubled by the old light. The voice had changed again, softening with the old lilt. 'It was a bit like dying, eh? Aye, a kind of death. But the skin kept walking – and filling up with hungers I could put no name to. There was a new thing growing in me, Robbie, creeping out of the darkness, gnawing like a worm in my guts.' His hand settled on Torrance's shoulder, lightly and lingeringly, playful and yet demanding. 'D'ye know what it was, Robbie?'

Torrance moved, and the hand fell away. He could not bear it and he could not meet the eyes. They were still on him. The laugh came, bleak and light.

'Aye, you know. You've always known. The good and godly Robert looking down from on high – and old Lije too.'

'Stay off from him!' The words came out of the sleep, deadly and flat, breaking the sleep. 'It was never a word I said to him – it was –'

'*And* your Maura!' The voice rose suddenly over him, savage with denial.

Torrance stood up, standing away. The sleep was over. The years and the freight of the years came washing in. They were themselves again. The smile was back, the cat voice played with him. 'So ye came out today to settle our business, did ye? I've waited long for it, Robbie. Why d'ye think I fiddled around with pan-flags – last year and this?'

151

'I knew.' The words came out of Torrance with cold quiet. There was finality and acceptance in them.

'And now what? Back to the ships for both of us, is it? – and then St. John's and the lawmen? Did ye ever expect that, Robbie? Did ye ever want it?'

There was a little stir on the pan in the middle of the lake. The big grey beasts were sniffing and turning uneasily, restless at the presence of men. Mahan's eyes travelled to them. 'It's a good place I found, with them out there,' he said mildly. 'From this spot, if one of us was to come back bleeding and one not come back, it could all be blamed on the Hoods.'

Torrance said nothing. Silence grew round them like a closing fist. The soft laugh broke it. 'Your Maura. Never a word of her yet – ye seem to avoid it. Is there nothing ye'd like to ask, Robbie – or be told? Teased ye about her, did I? – worried ye – just for the devil of it? God! – ' he was sudden and fierce again, 'did ye ever make yourself think it? – did ye think I'd stop there? Walking under those eyes of yours my life long – even when I did not know the thing that was in 'em – starved before fatness, stripped to the last rag? And now – *now*!'

He choked off the words and stood up, standing away too. The lips moved, the smile came twisting back. 'D'ye remember my first day home in St. John's, Robbie? – that day we met on the docks? – that afternoon we went for a walk on the hills?'

Torrance felt sweat beading his own face now. He would not think, he would not answer. But his voice came out, a husky, shaken whisper. 'I was glad enough to see you.'

'Aye.' The bitter laugh broke over him. 'But there were three years gone by then, and school-days done with, and we were both men grown. Men enough, anyway.'

Torrance was hardly conscious of any movement, but his feet were shifting back, testing the footing. The black eyes watched it all. The voice went on, uncoiling like a lash.

'Men enough, Robbie – the one of us, at least. Tall and clean with the pride of it all, weren't ye? Manhood too – ye'd kept that too – and ye spat in my face when I kissed ye!'

'For the love of God let be!' Torrance felt the cry torn out of him. He felt the last depths opened. The agony of that rejection lay on him, his agony, his guilt. His cry was a cry for mercy.

There was none in the black eyes. The lilt of the laugh broke, arid and harsh for once. 'The love of God! Aye, I knew that love – with the spittle wet on my cheek and the worm gnawing. I've lived with it ever since. It's made me. More than the other thing – ye know that, don't ye?'

He could not answer. There was no need. He did know.

'And what do I do now, Robbie? Live on with that blessed love, still knowing it? Aye, knowing the whole of it now, to the last black dregs.' The voice softened again, coiling again. 'What d'ye need to loose that hand of yours? The thought of the old one with the knife in his back? Or the thought of her – on the bed before the bride-bed?'

The words seemed somehow palpable, hung in the air. They were not yet fully through to Torrance's brain. The other voice cut through a mist. 'I spoiled her for ye – the day before the night. Ye've known, and not known. Ye've thought, and ye would not think, but it's all there. Shall I put it together for ye? Alone in the big house – three hours to wait – hot in her nakedness with the aunt gone out – and the south-side window open. Is it enough?'

The face came slowly clear to Torrance's eyes. The smile stiffened on the lips.

'Kiss me now, Robbie.'

Torrance lunged, and the flash of the gaff came streaking at him out of one rippling movement. The shaft whistled by, and he heard it shudder and sing as the point dug into the ice six feet behind him. Mahan was driving forward, but he had been pulled off balance by the throw; the lithe form straightened as he slipped and struggled to recover. Torrance drew back his arm, the gaff levelled at his shoulder, and suddenly the arm was water. He could not drive the steel head of that spear into the open throat. The shaft quivered in his grasp, and Mahan was onto him, knocking it out of his hand.

He heard it rattle to the ice. He felt the jolt come, padded by jacket and sweater, beating his ribs like a mallet, driving the breath from his lungs. His head snapped back and an elbow ground at his eye, then fists were rocking his head from side to side. He gave way, half-blinded, and a knee drove into his groin, doubling him up with the agony. He slipped to his knees, Mahan's hand came down on his neck, and flame-shot darkness seemed to explode in his brain. Groggy and bloody, staggering to his feet again, he went low for Mahan's knees. A boot came up for his chin but he managed to roll his head, and the boot glanced off with only a stab of pain. Then he had hold of the legs, locking them, and Mahan was wavering above him in a red mist.

He clung on savagely as the knees beat at his chest and the fists hammered his head, his shoulders, his neck. The knees gave, and Mahan toppled beneath him. But they struck at the edge of the ice and as Mahan kicked and squirmed, the two of them balanced precariously over a rim of black water. Torrance wrenched back, trying to roll Mahan with him, but he could not keep his grip. Doubling himself like a jack-knife, Mahan drove out with both feet, and the blow into Torrance's middle sent him skidding away on his back. He managed to turn, but he could not find his feet. He was still on his knees and swaying as Mahan loomed over him again, a block of ice in his hands. He started to straighten, slipped, and was on his knees again. For an instant a weird, cold, total calm came over him. The foot-square block was hovering above his head, he would feel the crash on his skull and nothing more.

But Mahan's towering form and bloody face were darkened by a shadow behind him. The shout that came, jerked out of Torrance's throat, stopped the other in his tracks and made him turn. The Hood, peering and sniffing, had come across the neck of ice. He was lifted high on his back flippers, his nostrils were dilating angrily, and his fore-flippers were beating the air not six feet from Mahan's shoulder-blades.

Mahan gave a sudden yell and let the ice block fly at the seal. It had been a startled, unthinking move, and it was a bad one. The chunk glanced off the armoured skull harmlessly, but it changed irritation to rage. The yapping bark gurgled low in the beast's throat, and, moving on the ice with twice the speed of a man, the seal lashed out with a flipper to open a long, ugly gash in Mahan's cheek. He reeled back, his head bobbing drunkenly from the blow, and as he did so the other flipper swept in with full force, knocking him to the ice.

Without taking time to get to his feet, Torrance slithered away, reaching for Mahan's gaff standing in the ice. He wrenched it free and turned, flinging it with all his strength, low at the belly of the seal. It struck and penetrated. The Hood gave a hoarse, bubbling whinny and turned away from Mahan with the gaff handle quivering in its front. There was time for Torrance to scramble to his own gaff now, and from his knees he drove it at the seal's eye. It missed, but still from his knees he plunged in beneath the flippers, gripped the shaft already shaking in the belly, and drove it home. The Hood, with a great, sighing screech, wobbled toward him in a red-streaming mass.

He pushed himself clear and straightened, steadying himself on his feet. Then he lunged in again, dodging the last, convulsive twitches, to drag the gaff from the body. The bitch had left the ice pan now. She was erect, shambling in with deceptive awkwardness, and he would have to deal with her. He ran to catch her at the edge of the water before she was thoroughly roused. The gaff plunged, but she was even quicker than her mate. He felt the shoulder of his jacket go, and then pain screamed through his body as her flipper tore away the flesh of his arm. He wrenched out the gaff and plunged it into her again and again. She quivered, settled on the ice with a weird, throaty, half-human moan, and it was over. Between the streaming bodies of the seals Mahan lay still unconscious. Torrance sank to his knees, deathly sick, clutching at his torn arm. He must not faint, something was telling him he must not faint.

At last he raised his head. The day had changed about him. He was hearing the warning sirens of the ships, and he realized that it had been a sound instinctively registering in his mind through all the fight.

He stumbled over to Mahan, dragged him half to his knees, let him slump back again as his own knees buckled to a wave of nausea. He heard his own voice, a shrill, gasping whisper, cursing himself for what he could not do. It would be so easy in this minute. The breathing carrion could be shoved to the edge of the ice, kicked into the black water like a skinned seal, and that would be the end. Instead he bent low, heaved the inert body to his shoulders, and swayed round from the lake to make for the foot of the ridge.

He fell as he reached it, and struggled upright again. Staggering and vomiting, grateful for the lightning flashes of pain that cleared his head, he clawed his way to the top, dragging Mahan after him. There was a steady trickle of fresh blood along the caked mass of his left arm, and he could feel the weakness growing in his middle. As he made the top of the ridge, heaved Mahan to his shoulders again, and stumbled toward the downward slope, he knew he was near his limit. The distant sound of the sirens was fading in his ears. At the brow of the slope he let Mahan slip to the ice, shaded his eyes, and peered off ahead of him, blinking and swaying. There was still gloomy afternoon light on the floe, but as he made out the ships in the distance he saw beyond them what he had expected to see. From the west, far out above the masts and funnels, there was a towering grey ridge, topped with light. The fog bank was sweeping in on them.

He tried to take Mahan to his shoulders again, but fell to his knees with the effort. Sprawled flat on his belly, he reached back, seized the bloody shoulder of the other's jacket, and inched the two of them forward and down. Head first, with jagged ice tearing at hands, faces, and knees, they reached the bottom of the slope and lay there. It was Mahan who stirred first. He sat up, turned his head toward Torrance, and glared at him for a moment with blank, foolish bewilderment. Then, as Torrance roused, the features drew together under the caked blood, the old eyes looked out at him. 'Ye should have finished me, Robbie.' It came in a hoarse whisper, and the eyes were changing again. Suddenly the cracked lips parted in a choking cry, 'Finish me now, ye fool!'

Torrance swayed to his feet and turned away from him. There was a dim commotion of voices and running men. He could make out a blur of faces, there were hands reaching out for him. A hand sent a flare of agony coursing the length of his arm, and he plunged forward into blackness.

S NOW-GLARE and cold gave way to steamy moonlight. Palms
drooped in a hot haze, rank port-smells drifted out. Surf
crashed, blue-white, round a white curve of sand. The snow-
glare came again, glaring it away. The saw-toothed floe rode
over it. Darkness was light and light was dark again, fire-gashed,
alive with tumult, thick with faces. Tall and at peace, with shining silence round it, the clock ticked softly in his father's parlour. The waves washed over it, the shadows yelled. The bed
before the bride-bed – the bed before the bride-bed. 'Finish me!'
– the eyes stared up from the huddle on the ice. A groan shook
Torrance, shuddering along the bunk. His eyes opened.

Lantern light. It was night, then. He was in his cabin, waiting. Time had slipped by, already too much time. White cloth
at his shoulder, bandages; his arm was throbbing beneath them.
Something he must do, something he must do. He started up and
sank back, his eyes on the bulkhead timbers. The thing was
sliding away from him; he was pushing it away.

The sense of the ship grew round him, heavy with disquiet
too. Instinct was nagging him awake. Overhead, familiar sounds
came to him with the eerie, muffled quality that all life takes on
in the midst of fog. He knew he was not alone and he moved at
last, shifting his eyes toward the door. Ernest Johns was standing
inside the cabin, his face shadowed and sombre in the dim light.
His pipe sucked noisily as he drew on it, and the gurgling had a
familiar realness that was somehow comforting. From the floe
outside, the ice noises and the distant bawling of the seals were
a muted background against which the creaking of the ship and
the stir of the men were a nearer play of shadow sound. Everything – ship and crew, the animal voices, and the moaning ice –

159

seemed trapped at the centre of a vast, malign silence that was swallowing the earth.

Johns took the pipe from his mouth as Torrance stirred. 'Ye've a bad gash in your shoulder,' he said, 'but it's clean now.'

Torrance groaned and struggled to sit up. He flinched at the heavy reproof in the old man's voice, yet something dead and inert in him still fought it. The pipe gurgled again on a strained silence, and its smoke mingled with the smells of coal and seal oil that filled the cabin to suffocation. 'Either ye should not have gone,' Johns said quietly at last, 'or he should not have come back. He walked to his ship; he's sound enough in his body. But neither his own men nor ours are safe now.'

Torrance sat silent, his knees hunched up under his chin, his face averted. The ship's bell struck. Time passing. There could not be much of it now. Something he must do. Something.

'Tomorrow, if the fog lifts,' Johns went on, 'we should clear out. Leave the pelts we haven't picked up. Holds are full and the deck pounds near full. Couldn't take more'n another three thousand anyway.'

Fog. Nothing to be done in fog. Torrance could not think. That hurrying stir within him would not move his body. The hard, serious eyes were on him. Johns was urgent, sure. He had talked it over with the watchmasters. Torrance quibbled, dully, idly.

'What about the men – if we run away from our pelts?'

'They'll go – and gladly. They want to get back with the fat we have, Robbie. They're not fooled by that talk of the Hoods out there. They've more'n an inkling of the truth of the business, and they want no more of it.'

No more of it. Torrance nodded, absorbing the words heavily, stupidly. 'Finish me!' the eyes had begged, glaring from the bloody face. 'Either ye should not have gone –' That haste, that numb stir was quickening in him again. But he let it go; he could focus his thoughts on nothing. There was only the throb of his arm and the nakedness and emptiness within him, utter and complete now. Maura – she had come to him under that white veil with Mahan's bruises black on her flesh, she had stood at the altar with his breath in her nostrils still, the feel of him in

160

her loins. Maura – Maura – suddenly the thought engulfed all other thoughts, flung him from side to side like a rising sea, and lifted him at last, incredibly, on a swell of release and joy. Maura – it had been Mahan's doing, not hers. Nothing had ever been changed in her, nothing lost. Maura –

'Finish me!' It was finished. He started up, free and alive, whole again, and suddenly shaken by a startled hope. Two choices, he had said – two choices. Clear out of the patch, be ten miles off by morning. Something was moving, changing in the ice. There was a new commotion stirring over his head. The random shuffle of boots had become a flow, crowding to the port bulwark. There was a muted babble of questionings, and then a shout or two, anxious and sharp.

'Fog cleared?' Johns was alert and tense, answering his own question. 'Can't be that. Gave no sign of it ten minutes ago.'

There was another shout, and he swung round for the doorway. But Torrance was already ahead of him, clattering up the ladder.

Jean Bright lay with her starboard side just off the edge of the floe. The men along the port bulwark were looking out toward open water, arguing and pointing. The loudest were insisting that they had seen something off amid the fog to port. ''Twas a light, sor!' one of them shouted to Torrance as he pushed into the huddle, 'I seen a masthead light hard by!' Another raised a hand and cupped it to his ear. 'Listen!' he bellowed, and a hush fell over the deck.

There was a sound in the water out beyond them, near. Then came other sounds. They were hearing a ship's engines and the crash of a sealer's bow smashing through loose ice.

Hardy's voice snapped out with tense anger. *'Kestrel!* They're mad, all of 'em, this trip. Moving off in fog. 'Twill be the death of her!'

'And a good t'ing.' Another grizzled outport man ground his pipe-stem between his teeth. 'Sarve her right. Sarve Tim Mahan right, and the fools that sailed wit' him. Jinker, he is!'

Suddenly the mutterings of the men forward changed to hoarse yells. They were followed by an echoing roar from the whole crew. Immense, vague, a giant ship in the magnifying

161

particles of the fog bank, *Kestrel* stood up, bow on, bearing down on them. Every voice on the deck was shrill with warning, Johns had already set off the blare of the siren, but the great shape came on unwaveringly. Its hugeness lessened as it cut clear of the fog, grew again as the mist wreathed about it, then narrowed to a looming wedge crawling forward with deadly menace.

For a moment Torrance stood dazed as his mind swung to the meaning. Then he was up on the bulwark, bellowing the hopeless order at the other ship. 'Astern! Full astern!' The laugh came through the fog, faint and familiar; the only answer, and it told all. There was nothing to do, no possible way of avoiding the blow. The shouts fell away, breathlessly. Over the slosh of water, the suck of ice, there seemed to be utter silence, and then the shock came. *Kestrel's* iron bow crashed into *Jean Bright* amidships, rode up high, grating along the double-timbered bulwarks, then slid off sidewise as they splintered but stood fast. Struggling to his feet among a sprawling, yelling tangle of men knocked flat by the impact, Torrance was dimly aware that the same sounds of panic were coming from *Kestrel*. Her bow was pulling off as he fought his way to the port bulwark again, but even before he reached it there was the renewed roaring of steam. She was coming in once more. Men staggered back on him, their arms before their faces, knocking him to the deck, sprawling on top of him. There was a new shudder, and the sagging bulwark gave, bent inward. The iron wedge was not sheering off this time; it was biting into the side, fastening its grip.

Fighting off arms and legs, staggering erect again, Torrance felt the port side lifting with the thrust. Men were screaming and grabbing at each other as they lost their footing with the rise, sliding to starboard along the oily, tilting planks. *Jean Bright,* with her holds packed and tons of pelts piled high on her deck, was heeling drunkenly. She shivered, made as if to come upright, and then the timbers of the deck pounds gave. The crash of baulks and the rubbery gurgle of sliding pelts was followed by a tearing of bulkheads in the hold below as irresistible weight surged against them. The whole tonnage of fat was shifting.

The ship fell over to starboard, taking on a sagging dead-

162

ness as water climbed and lapped across the bulwark. Jagged sticks of timber, loose mounds of pelts, and tangled masses of men slithering helplessly down the canting deck added to the weight of the water. As the crew tumbled over the side, arms flailing, heads bobbing among the washing pans of ice, the starboard bulwark went under. Fittings gave way on board; there was a crash and a gush of flame as the galley stove dumped its live coals into a river of running fat. Men who gained the solid edge of the floe turned to watch, helpless and sickened, as fires flared briefly and were smothered by engulfing water. They heard the dull rush of the last pelts released from the breaking pounds, and then a low, gurgling roar as the boilers exploded. The mast-peaks swept downward, cutting a great, slow arc through the fog. They came level with the ice and rested for a moment quivering on its edge. Then they broke through or splintered, and amid a lashing hail of ice fragments and flying wood *Jean Bright* turned over and sank.

A hundred yards back from the lip of ice where the ship had gone under, Torrance stood while the men huddled about him. Names were passing in the gloom. The watchmasters were calling their rolls as well as they could from memory. Fifteen or twenty names were repeated, passing from lip to lip, and no voice answered. There were men going down with the hulk settling in the depths, others in the water still churning round it. The rest stood helpless without food or gear, everything they had come for gone, and everything that might take them home with their lives.

Johns came up to Torrance as the roll-call dwindled off. The sound of *Kestrel*'s engines was growing fainter in the fog. When he spoke, the words came as though they were not his own, as though he were reading them in some cold book of doom. 'It was Mahan alone,' he said, 'Tim Mahan that ordered up the steam and came in on us in the fog and rammed us. Tim Mahan giving the steering-orders and no man else in the ship knowing what he was about.'

The mist stirred to a chill breath, swirled upward in lightening wreaths. Johns looked at the sky and sniffed the wind. 'Changing,' he said. 'Veering to the nor'west.'

His voice had grown almost gentle, with the clear certainty

163

of the child. Assenting now, the last of his doubts gone. He knew what was to be, and he saw the shape of it.

For at the break of the bitter morning the wind was blowing sharp from the north-west, and the outward channels of the floe had closed in, iron-hard. *Kestrel* lay two miles off, locked in from open water. Already the ridges that had beaten her back were piling up ahead of her, and the whole face of the floe was alive with slithering pans, hurled in like huge projectiles by the force of wind and swell.

Her men were out on the ice, fore and aft of her, and to leeward, with axes and ice-chisels and hawsers and dynamite, but their work was useless there. The trap had closed on her to windward, and on the windward side no man could live. It was a fog of flying chips and powdering snow, through which the charging ice blocks drove at the hull. If they climbed above the bulwarks or stove them in, funnel and masts would snap. The ship would drift to its end, already dead, buried in the heart of the floe.

Around Torrance the men straightened to their feet in silence, their ice-glazed pants and jackets crackling as they moved. He swung his arms and beat them against his sides, waking the flare of pain in his gashed arm as the blood stirred again. It quickened the aching numbness of body and mind, and his guilt was a stone within him. But the thing he had not done was still to do, and it came before the saving of that locked-in ship, for all else depended on it. The purpose was sure in him as he started on his way against the lashing wind and the skidding fragments of ice. He could not bring himself to speak, but the men streamed behind him, heads bent against the gale, carrying the few poor tools that had lain near to their hands as they tumbled out of the ship. They knew, he thought, as he worked his stiff fingers round the splintered stick of timber he had picked up from the ice. They knew what must be done and they would do it if he did not. But he would not fail them twice.

He passed among the *Kestrel* men working on the ice, and without looking he felt them draw aside and leave a lane for him. Their faces, he knew, like the faces of those behind him would wear that stony calm. He climbed over the lee bulwark of

the ship with his own men swarming after him and the circle of
Kestrel's men quietly closing from the ice. Already the ship was
heeling from the pressure against her windward side, and the
men on deck were clinging to the fittings and the pounds to keep
their feet.

Alone on the fo'c's'le head, apart from all his crew, Mahan
had been watching as Torrance came over the side. Now he was
moving. The gaff swung in his hand, a knife was stuck in his
belt, and he came down the listing deck with quick, careful steps
to where Torrance waited. No man of either crew stirred a foot
to come between them. Instead, the nearest men shuffled back,
crowding back those behind them, to clear the open space between the lee bulwark and the pound. Amid the gale, the sway
of movement gathering along the deck and gathering in from
the ice, was a soundless, inexorable thing, a multiplying of eyes,
steely, intent, assenting.

The two in the cleared space circled each other as the ice
thundered against the ship and the wind howled along the deck.
The thing would be swift, for there was now no flaw in either of
hope or mercy. Their eyes met as they moved, always nearing,
and there was only acceptance in them.

'Time for it, eh Robbie?' Mahan spoke for Torrance alone.
'High time, Tim.'

Suddenly Mahan lunged, driving his gaff for the throat, and
Torrance swung his club to break the gaff from the hand and
break the wrist with it. Mahan's right arm dropped to his side,
but he plunged in, with the fingers of his left hand clutching for
the knife in his belt. The knife came free, but it slipped from his
fumbling fingers. He turned, dived after it, and it skidded beyond his reach. Half-sprawling, doubled on all fours, he spun
round again to tear off his cap and fling it at Torrance's eyes.
Then he followed it in.

The club came down once more, driving at the charging
knees, but Torrance stumbled with the cap in his eyes. A searing
shock ran up the length of his arm as Mahan kicked the club
from his hands. Mahan's left hand was at his throat, bending him
backward. He gasped and beat out with his fists but could not
break that terrible, single-handed grip. His eyes were starting

165

from their sockets and his tongue forcing its way between his teeth when his fingers, groping for Mahan's shattered wrist, found it and twisted with all the strength he had left. Mahan gave a strangled scream and Torrance wrenched away. Diving under the arm, scrambling along the deck, he reached the club. He turned, swinging low for the knees again, and the shudder of the impact ran the length of his arms. He heard through blinding pain the crack of the wood, the crack of the breaking bones. Then, as Mahan's trunk crumpled onto the shattered legs, he raised the stump of the club for the last time and brought it down with all the hate that was in him on the black head.

As he bent over the smashed thing quivering on the deck before him, his eyes cleared. He saw the line of the neck beneath the jacket collar. A shaggy curl twisted down over the young flesh, untouched by the clotting ooze above. Suddenly a terrible haste possessed him. He lifted the body in his arms, staggered up the deck through an opening lane of men, and with a great, sobbing heave flung it over the windward bulwark. He saw the groaning, tortured mass of the ice, reddening as it took its offering to itself. Then new pans thundered in to grind it among them, and cover it from sight.

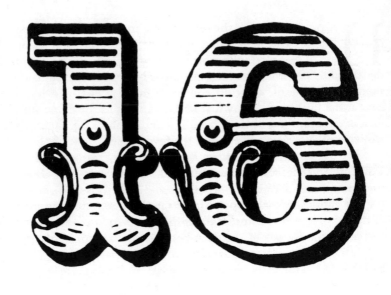

HE swayed, and for the second time in two days blackness engulfed him. It came and went, gave way and came again, peopled with horrors. He was dimly aware, amid the stalking nightmares, that time passed. He was conscious of shouts and turmoil, of wind and battering ice. His own hand beat at the bulkhead, his own voice cried out, but the flame-shot mist of delirium was always there. It was the fourth day when he woke from a sweating sleep with the fever gone.

Hardy sat by the bunk in *Kestrel's* cabin, Mahan's cabin. Told off for the watch, he confessed. For seventy-two hours there had been one man always there and sometimes two, holding the captain down. Above him through those hours the men of the two crews had emptied the ship. They had heaved over the last pelts, the frames of the deck pounds, the last sticks of timber, building a flimsy rampart to ward off the charging ice. They had pecked hopelessly with their tools and dynamite at the ridges rising round them, only to find the prison locking closer. Yet – Torrance looked up with his cracked lips framing a question – the ship was in motion now.

Hardy nodded. It was just three hours before that the wind had swung and the sea changed. The locked-in ship and the ice itself had been lifted with a mighty, crackling heave, and the crash of breaking channels had run away toward the horizon. Torrance could feel the shudder of the engines now and hear the splash of free water against the bow. *Kestrel* was labouring out through a crack in the floe, heavy with the weight of four hundred men returning poorer than they came. And that was the least of the burden.

For an hour after Hardy left him, Torrance lay still. Then

he sat up and swung his feet to the deck. The thought of those faces above had haunted the mists of delirium. There was still dread and doubt as he groped round for his sea-gear, struggled painfully into it, and dragged himself to the companionway.

The haggard, comprehending face of Ernest Johns met him as he came topside. Johns's hand was on his arm as he limped across the deck through the parted sea of his judges. He raised his head to look about him, over all the men of the two crews, solid from bulwark to bulwark. There was no accusal there, only a solemn understanding. Hands and voices reached out to him in sober greeting, forging the link, sharing the weight. It could be borne now.

They were five days to the western edge of the floe. Battered and wrenched, leaking from every seam, the ship swung southward into the choppy swells of the Cut. On the twelfth day, with sirens mute and a black flag flying at the peak, *Kestrel* crawled in through the Narrows.

From the deck Torrance could see the streets begin to fill, emptying themselves toward the water. The sound of voices came out, low and subdued; everyone knew there would be bells tolling this night. There was a murmur of surprise as the Playfair ship put in at the Bracebridge jetty, and a louder murmur as Torrance limped down the gangway. The air filled with questions but he did not try to answer them, for he had no comfort. Friends put out their hands but he brushed by unseeing, and they let him go. All up the length of Water Street the crowd parted round him, and sober faces looked after him as he turned to the path for home.

As he rounded the last bend and the wind from the hill struck him, there was a flat clack of wood. The house door was swinging open. Maura was beyond the house, standing on the edge of the cliff, looking out to the sea. She seemed to have been there always, looking for nothing; there was no youth in the lines of that young body, no hope in the bowed shoulders.

Somehow in the droop of those shoulders, in the whining wind, and the aimless clatter of wood, there was final desolation. The years-to-be marched over him, crumbling him under their weight. The house crumbled, sagging on rotted timber, mutter-

170

ing with falling stone. He saw with the unborn eyes that would come to see it the gaping windows and the parting ribs of the walls, the thrust of sand and weed through heaved-up planks. Salt-grey, rain-black, the tumbling rubble sank, gnawing into the hill-side. The rock stood bare again, even the memory gone, blown from it, washed from it, buried under it, gone with the million winds, the endless passing.

He brushed a hand across his eyes, faint and sick. The house still stood. She was waiting on the cliff. Their time was here about them, still to be lived. He moved out to her and she turned slowly, hearing his step. Suddenly her eyes grew wide. Her hands went to her face and she was swaying on her feet as he caught her, and it was only then that the thought came to him of what she would have seen.

'*Kestrel*!' she gasped. 'It was *Kestrel* coming back –'

'Aye. But not Mahan.' He could spare her nothing; the weight was hers too. 'He's gone. And *Jeannie* with him. And eighteen of the lads I might have saved. My work, all of it.'

'No!' She clung to him and shivered as the words sank in on her. '*My* work!' She settled down on the rock, and the long, dissolving shudder was like that other settling. The anguish before him was like the other anguish. The same pity ached in him. He raised her gently at last, and she looked up.

'My work,' she repeated, 'for it was I who let you go. I sent you.'

'No.'

His hands closed on her shoulders but she seemed to shrink away from them, her eyes wide. 'Eighteen men –'

'And him,' he said. 'A man too.'

Her head sank with the words and the strange quiet of the tone. 'Yes.' Out of a long pause her voice came very softly. 'He told you, then. You know.'

It was not a question. She looked up, searching his face, waiting. Only her eyes and body questioned him now, her whole being.

He took her in his arms and his body closed against her and she was answered. No joy yet, but joy would come. He looked out above her head, holding her, warm with her warmth. Below

171

her were the rocks, and the sea lay blue beyond, blue and smiling, flecked with glittering white. The floe crawled down to the sun and dissolution, creeping to return again, water and snow again, bound in the iron rhythm. The house still stood. The wind that clacked the door lifted her sunny hair, brushing his cheek. Their time was here about them, broadening in sunlight.

They would speak of it later in peace, and there would be no freedom. They were part of it all, they would carry it all still, the stout ship sucking down in the black water, the roll-call in the windy night, the silences, the beaded face on the ice, the crumpled thing on the deck, the dark curl, the white line of the flesh beneath the jacket collar – all to be lived with still. No freedom yet, no wish for freedom now. Peace was enough to build on, peace, bare peace.

She looked up, seeing it in his eyes, accepting it. No freedom, only peace. Only the hard, spent calm of the great ice moving with the great current on the breast of the greater sea. He turned her gently toward the open doorway.